CRIME STRIKES A CHORD

SCHOOL OF HARD ROCKS, BOOK 2

CHRISTY BARRITT

COMPLETE BOOK LIST

Squeaky Clean Mysteries:

#1 Hazardous Duty

#2 Suspicious Minds

#2.5 It Came Upon a Midnight Crime (novella)

#3 Organized Grime

#4 Dirty Deeds

#5 The Scum of All Fears

#6 To Love, Honor and Perish

#7 Mucky Streak

#8 Foul Play

#9 Broom & Gloom

#10 Dust and Obey

#11 Thrill Squeaker

#11.5 Swept Away (novella)

#12 Cunning Attractions

#13 Cold Case: Clean Getaway

#14 Cold Case: Clean Sweep

#15 Cold Case: Clean Break

#16 Cleans to an End

While You Were Sweeping, A Riley Thomas Spinoff

The Sierra Files:

#1 Pounced

#2 Hunted

#3 Pranced

#4 Rattled

The Gabby St. Claire Diaries (a Tween Mystery series):

The Curtain Call Caper

The Disappearing Dog Dilemma

The Bungled Bike Burglaries

The Worst Detective Ever

#1 Ready to Fumble

#2 Reign of Error

#3 Safety in Blunders

#4 Join the Flub

#5 Blooper Freak

#6 Flaw Abiding Citizen

#7 Gaffe Out Loud

#8 Joke and Dagger

#9 Wreck the Halls

#10 Glitch and Famous

Raven Remington

Relentless 1

Relentless 2 (coming soon)

Holly Anna Paladin Mysteries:

#1 Random Acts of Murder

#2 Random Acts of Deceit

#2.5 Random Acts of Scrooge

#3 Random Acts of Malice

#4 Random Acts of Greed

#5 Random Acts of Fraud

#6 Random Acts of Outrage

#7 Random Acts of Iniquity

Lantern Beach Mysteries

#1 Hidden Currents

#2 Flood Watch

#3 Storm Surge

#4 Dangerous Waters

#5 Perilous Riptide

#6 Deadly Undertow

Lantern Beach Romantic Suspense

Tides of Deception

Breakwater Protector

Cape Corral Keeper

Seagrass Secrets

Driftwood Danger

Beach House Mysteries

The Cottage on Ghost Lane

Carolina Moon Series

Home Before Dark

Gone By Dark

Wait Until Dark

Light the Dark

Taken By Dark

Suburban Sleuth Mysteries:

Death of the Couch Potato's Wife

Fog Lake Suspense:

Edge of Peril

Margin of Error

Brink of Danger

Line of Duty

Cape Thomas Series:

Dubiosity

Disillusioned

Distorted

Standalone Romantic Mystery:

The Good Girl

Suspense:

Imperfect

The Wrecking

Sweet Christmas Novella:

Home to Chestnut Grove

Standalone Romantic-Suspense:

Keeping Guard

The Last Target

Race Against Time

Ricochet

Key Witness

Lifeline

High-Stakes Holiday Reunion

Desperate Measures

Hidden Agenda

Mountain Hideaway

Dark Harbor

Shadow of Suspicion

The Baby Assignment

The Cradle Conspiracy

Trained to Defend

Mountain Survival

Nonfiction:

Characters in the Kitchen

Changed: True Stories of Finding God through Christian Music (out of print)

The Novel in Me: The Beginner's Guide to Writing and Publishing a Novel (out of print)

CHAPTER ONE

HAD *my husband been cheating on me?*

The question echoed in my mind until I couldn't think about anything else. I wanted to believe I was wrong . . . but did the evidence I'd found prove otherwise?

Phil . . . you wouldn't do that to me . . . right?

"Camryn? What do you think?"

I snapped back to reality and glanced at my assistant, who, based on the way she stared at me now, had most likely been talking to me. "What?"

"You've *got* to help the Abernathys," Skittles said. "You did such an amazing job after the school's last murder mystery."

I frowned as I sat in my office. The last murder mystery? Skittles' words made the whole ordeal sound so tame, like students had been playing a game. In reality, people had died. *Real* people.

I stared at my assistant. Her official name was Professor Skittles. The college junior had legally changed her name, probably as an attention grab or in an effort to get her superiors to call her "professor." Either way, the name fit Skittles, with her colorful hair and even more colorful clothing.

As "I'll Be Home for Christmas" drifted through the small speaker on the bookshelf behind me, I crossed my arms and glanced from my assistant to Chancellor Joseph Hannon, my boss.

Even though it was a Saturday, we had only one week of school before Christmas break. Most faculty and staff members were working this weekend to get everything done so they could enjoy their time off.

If I was reading the room correctly, both Skittles and Joseph were waiting for my response to Skittles' plea for me to help her friends by investigating.

"Solving those murders back in October was just a fluke," I insisted. "I couldn't re-create those detective skills if I tried."

"It wasn't a fluke." Skittles popped a red piece of candy into her mouth. "You were *brilliant*. Everyone thinks so."

I blushed at the compliment. I hadn't expected to feel such fulfillment after solving a crime. But I had.

I was supposed to be a fixer. I came into businesses and organizations in need of image control, and I cleaned things up. I just hadn't expected solving a murder to be a part of the job description. But since coming to my alma mater, Grand Isle Music Conservatory, that seemed to be the case.

Joseph straightened and squared his rounded shoulders. "I personally think it's a great idea."

I turned to my boss and former classmate, my eyebrows flinging toward the ceiling. "What?"

Certainly, I hadn't heard him correctly. Because anyone in their right mind could see this was a very bad idea.

"You solving that last case did great things for our school's reputation—which is exactly why we hired you." Joseph's eyes gleamed with excitement, like his out-of-the-box thinking could make him an innovator among his peers. "Any more feathers in our cap would be appreciated. We have *a lot* to make up for."

That was true, I supposed. I'd been hired here at Grand Isle in Savannah, Georgia, to do damage control after a rash of bad decisions and unfortunate situations—including more than one murder. I needed to help make the institution respectable again.

I sighed and leaned back in my desk chair,

ignoring the carrots and mustard I'd just begun snacking on before my office was invaded.

My gaze flickered up to my assistant. I might as well find out more information. "Skittles, tell me one more time what happened to your friends."

Skittles' eyes lit with excitement as if she'd just been waiting for the chance to talk about it again. "The Abernathys—"

"Are one of our top donors," Joseph cut in, leaning forward as if to drive home his point. His robust belly, circular face, and bald head only added to his former opera singer persona.

"They recently moved here from Florida, so they hired a moving company to help them." Skittles' voice dropped low. "But their belongings never made it to their new home."

"What happened?" I continued to listen, curious as to where she was going with this.

"That's the thing. No one knows." Skittles shrugged dramatically, a natural storyteller who might want to consider acting if her music career didn't work out. "This moving company stopped answering their phone. The address where their business was supposed to be located didn't actually exist."

"That's unfortunate."

"I know what you're thinking—that the family

was naive or too trusting. But the Abernathys are smart. She was a professional musician, and he's a real estate mogul who's made millions. These people did their research. So, whoever's behind this crime is also smart—smart enough to have pulled the wool over their eyes."

The incident sounded deplorable, but tracking missing possessions didn't exactly excite me. However, I did have a few more questions, just to satisfy my curiosity before I said no.

"What are these people doing with the Abernathys' possessions? Selling them?"

"Here's the thing." Skittles' eyes lit. "It turns out, this isn't the first time something like this has happened. These con artists hold people's possessions hostage and demand a ransom. When the family pays up, they send information on where the family's belongings can be found. These people, the victims, will pay whatever these crooks ask—especially considering the heirlooms that have been hijacked. This has been happening all over the Southeast coast."

I shook my head as I thought about my own belongings. I didn't have much that I was sentimental about, but there were a few things—photos, some jewelry, the Grammy I'd won for best new female artist nearly twenty years ago.

Some people would call that my heyday. I called it another chapter in my life.

"Criminals just keep getting more and more clever, don't they?" I finally muttered. "But I'm not sure how I can help with this. It sounds like a police matter."

"There's more." Skittles held up a finger, her eyes still dancing. "In fact, this is where it gets interesting. The Abernathys have a Stradivari violin that's been handed down for generations. It's missing."

"They put a priceless violin in a moving truck?" Had I heard correctly? Skittles said these people were smart—but that decision didn't seem wise. People didn't just hand Stradivaris over to strangers.

"The violin wasn't supposed to go onto the truck," Skittles said. "But after the movers left, Mrs. Abernathy realized it was missing from the closet where she kept it."

The song playing on the small speaker changed to Elvis' "Blue Christmas." The shift somehow seemed appropriate for this conversation.

"How much are we talking about this violin being worth?" I shifted my weight in my chair as I listened. I knew a little about Stradivaris, but not enough to form a clear picture.

"Two million."

My eyes widened at that figure. "I knew a Stradivari was worth a lot, but that's a *ton* of money."

"Tell me about it. But it's not the money that concerns the Abernathys the most. It's the sentimental value of the instrument."

I studied Skittles' face another moment as I tried to formulate my response. This seemed really important to her, but I wasn't sure why she was so invested. Was she simply bored and looking for more material to place on her social media?

"How do you know this family, exactly?" I asked.

"Their daughter, Tara, is one of my best friends. She graduated from Grand Isle last year. Anyway, she just got accepted into the Detroit Symphony Orchestra, and she was hoping to finally be able to play her family's violin. It's all she's wanted to do for years."

I let out a sigh. This whole thing seemed like something the police should be able to handle—much more so than I could. After all, I was merely a former singer turned public relations expert. Just because my father was a famous con artist, my brother a former detective, and my deceased husband the head of a security firm didn't make me an authority.

"This mystery sounds fascinating, but I'm still not

sure how I can help. Tracking down stolen items isn't my specialty." None of this was, to be honest.

I just needed to write press releases and plan special programs for donors. In fact, Christmas was only three weeks away. In one week, right before Winter Break, students at the school were performing at our biggest fundraiser of the year. I needed to concentrate my time on that.

"You and your supersonic hearing could definitely be valuable," Joseph added with a knowing nod.

I tilted my head as I gave Joseph a skeptical look. "It's not supersonic."

I had both hyperacusis and complex echoic memory, which meant, in simple terms, that I heard things most people didn't. I could also memorize sounds—almost like a photographic memory, but with noise instead of images. Often, I could hear when someone was lying, just by listening to changes in their tone.

Sometimes, sounds overwhelmed me and overloaded my senses, but I'd learned to control my response to too many audio stimuli. Still, keeping myself in check was an ongoing process.

"Anyway, this violin has a distinct woody, round sound," Skittles continued. "If someone buys the instrument and plays it, maybe you could listen and pick it out in the crowd."

I shook my head as I imagined myself doing that. It *might* be possible—but what were the odds I'd go somewhere someone was playing this violin?

"I like how you're thinking." I tried to keep my tone gentle. "But who knows how many concerts I'd have to go to in order to identify the sound? If these people are smart, they'll try to sell the instrument to someone in Europe or Asia. How would I find it then? I can't exactly travel the world looking for it."

Skittles frowned and sagged against the wall as if she hadn't thought about that angle. "You're right. It was just an idea."

As Skittles said the words, her phone rang. She put it to her ear and took a few steps away. Her voice seemed to grow louder—and more urgent—with every response.

Joseph and I exchanged a look.

Was something wrong?

A moment later, Skittles lowered her phone and turned toward us. "You'll never believe this."

My heart thrummed as I waited for her to continue. I didn't want to be curious, but I was.

"That was Barbara Abernathy," Skittles continued. "She said the police just called and told her they found a box from their moving truck."

"Was their stuff still inside the box?" I asked.

"Yes, it was full of their belongings."

"That's great news." Joseph's voice lifted.

"But there's more." Skittles frowned. "A dead body was found beside it."

My breath caught.

A dead body?

That revelation just took this investigation to an entirely different level.

———

I shouldn't be here. Every instinct inside me made that clear.

Yet here I was.

At the crime scene.

With Skittles as well as Mrs. Abernathy.

Apparently, Barbara Abernathy wasn't only a big donor to Grand Isle but also to the police fund. That had somehow allowed her the privilege of coming to the scene when most others wouldn't have been notified.

Skittles had driven me to a back alley in Savannah, a narrow place sandwiched between a startup bakery and a sketchy comic shop. The space was just like every alley I'd ever pictured—dirty, smelly, and dimly lit, with two dumpsters and litter scrambling along the brick-stoned walkway.

Except, in this alley, there was a dead body, multiple police officers, and crime-scene tape that flapped with the gentle, trash-tinged breeze. A car sped past in the distance blaring hip-hop music. Someone inside the bakery shouted instructions, probably from the kitchen as some kind of machinery was turned on.

There were so many sounds around me—signs of life continuing on despite tragedy.

The police clustered near the body, Skittles talked to Mrs. Abernathy near one of the dumpsters, and a small crowd had gathered on the sidewalk behind me.

I pressed my lips together as I tried to look composed. Instead, I felt like a wannabe Nancy Drew showing up here.

I felt even more like a wannabe when I saw Detective Garrison. The man was in his early thirties, with dark hair and a quiet demeanor. The two of us had worked together on a previous case.

Worked together was probably a strong way to word it, however. But I *had* helped when he'd gotten stuck while solving the murder of a Grand Isle student. That had to count for something.

"Camryn Paine . . . what brings you here?" He paused in front of me, an unreadable look in his dark eyes as he peered at me.

The edge in his voice indicated I wasn't welcome. I could understand why the police didn't want everyday citizens here at the crime scene.

Despite that, I shrugged as if my presence were no big deal. "Just another day at the office."

He grunted. "You know the Abernathys?"

"As a matter of fact . . ." I started to say I was connected with them but changed my mind and shook my head apologetically instead. "As a matter of fact, no. I don't."

He shifted, one hand jangling some coins in his pocket. "So, really . . . why are you here?"

I let out a sigh, wondering how exactly I should explain this. Before I could say anything, someone stepped up beside me.

"I invited her to come here." Barbara Abernathy's commanding presence took center stage in the alley, her upright stance and confident voice making it clear she was a force to be reckoned with. "This woman is quite remarkable."

"She is." Garrison cast me a look that I wasn't sure how to read.

Partial agreement? Partial annoyance?

Most likely.

Mrs. Abernathy was in her sixties, and her shockingly dark hair stood out against pale skin. She was thin and wore skintight leather pants, high heels, and pearls. Her upturned expression dared anyone to defy her.

"Do you have any idea who this man was?" Barbara turned back to Detective Garrison and nodded toward the dead body, which had been draped with a cloth.

The man lay sprawled on the dirty bricks between the two dumpsters. Yellow placards had been placed strategically around the area to notate possible evidence. A forensic photographer documented the scene.

"We're still trying to ID him," Garrison said. "It appears he died of a head wound."

"Anyone nearby hear an argument?" I felt like it wasn't my place to ask, but I didn't regret the question. There was a good possibility I could help here— if I decided I wanted to do that.

"No." Garrison frowned. "Unfortunately, there weren't any Camryn Paines nearby to offer their insight at the time of the crime."

I nodded slowly, wondering if that was a subtle jab or a compliment. Garrison was hard to read.

Just then, another officer called Garrison to the body. The man held a cell phone in his gloved hand.

As Garrison went to check it out, I crept closer to hear what they were saying.

"We found this in his pocket," the officer said.

"There's nothing on it other than a voice mail. No fingerprints. No photos. No saved contacts. No outgoing calls. Clearly a burner."

"Play the voice mail," Garrison said.

I leaned closer, an intrinsic part of me wanting to hear.

"You don't want to do this," a man growled over the recording. "Believe me, you don't."

Then the voice mail ended.

But there was more to that message than the man's gruff voice.

A background noise caught my ear.

A bird.

Not just any bird—a parrot.

Garrison studied me. "What did you hear? Don't say it wasn't anything. I can see it in your eyes."

I nibbled on my bottom lip before admitting, "A parrot. There's a parrot in the background of that voice mail."

His eyebrows shot up. "You're sure?"

"Nearly certain. Birds have different songs and tones, just like people have different voices."

He continued to stare at me as if skeptical.

I shrugged. "Growing up, my mom had a parrot. I know what one sounds like."

Finally, he nodded, his shoulders seeming to loosen. "Good work."

I smiled, happy my blessing/curse could help.

Unfortunately, that's how I viewed my abilities. I knew my supersonic hearing—as Joseph called it—allowed me to notice things others didn't. But sometimes, even though I'd mostly learned to control it, it was difficult to turn my listening skills off. Instead, it sounded like a million different noises crashed together inside my head. Sometimes, I wanted to place my hands over my ears and sink into the corner in an effort to disappear, to find some peace.

In my life, that wasn't an option. I'd taught my daughter, Scarlett, to never give up on things that were important to her—and I needed to live that out also.

"If we need more help . . ." Garrison's voice trailed.

His words made me feel more satisfied than I should. "Just let me know."

I glanced at my watch and sighed. I had just enough time to make it to my meeting with Weston Turner—a professor at the conservatory. The two of us had been assigned to work together on the holiday program, and we needed to discuss some final details.

Working with him excited me a little more than it should.

But it was just because I'd always been a sucker

for cowboys—not because I once thought the two of us were destined to be together.

WESTON STOOD as I stepped into his office a little later. "Camryn . . . you're looking cheery. I like red on you."

I'd dressed for Christmas today in a red shirt and black plaid skirt. "Thank you."

I leaned close enough for him to give me a kiss on the cheek.

That polite little kiss shouldn't bring me nearly as much pleasure as it did, nor should feeling the prickle from his barely-there beard.

I pushed a blonde hair behind my ear and lowered myself into the chair across from him, attempting to look like the picture of a professional, poised, and platonic friend.

But it was hard to be those things around your first love and the man who'd broken your heart—

even if more than twenty years had passed since then.

Weston leaned back casually in his chair with his cowboy-boot-clad feet propped on his desk. He was a western rock singer and the consummate country boy—except he had swagger and made women's hearts melt with his swoon-worthy lyrics, a honey-filled voice, and a drop-dead gorgeous smile. His reddish-brown hair was still thick, and he kept himself in shape, possibly because it was expected of him as a performer and possibly because he was just one of those guys.

"I think we should talk about the Christmas program somewhere more casual," Weston started. "This place feels too much like work, doesn't it? And The Christmas Thing is entirely more than that."

The students had named the annual Christmas event here at the conservatory. In its own way, the name was brilliant. Simple. Effective. To the point. Memorable.

"I'm going to have to say no—unless you suggest we get beignets at Bartholomew's." I picked the location only for the food, not because the cafe had been a turning point in our relationship a couple of months ago.

It was while eating there with Weston that I knew I could work with my former boyfriend here at the conservatory without being thrown off balance or sent into an emotional torpedo.

I was forty-three. A widow. An empty-nester. A former music star.

Yet sometimes I didn't feel as if I knew who I was at all.

Especially now that I worried my husband had been cheating on me. Were things between the two of us not as happy as I'd assumed? Had I been blind to what was really going on in Phil's life?

I'd recently found some emails between Phil and a woman named Andrea. Reading them had thrown doubt on me like a wet blanket. What exactly had their relationship been?

"You know I'm always up for beignets. Let's go." Weston stood and grabbed his black leather jacket.

We started out the door toward his truck in the parking lot.

It wasn't until we were inside the vehicle that Weston said, "I heard you're helping with another investigation."

I balked. "What? How did you hear that?"

"Word travels fast around Grand Isle." He grinned.

"No, really. How did you hear?" Having people know I was possibly helping with police investigations didn't necessarily work in my favor. In fact, it could make me a target.

Weston shrugged as if it wasn't a big deal. "Skittles, of course. I ran into her earlier, and she filled me in."

I grunted. I'd have to have a talk with her about that later.

We headed down the road. Bartholomew's wasn't far away. But since time wasn't on our side, we'd decided to drive.

I rubbed the smooth leather of my purse as I rested it in my lap and finally said, "For the record, I never agreed to help with the investigation."

"But you will."

I scoffed. "You think you know me so well."

"You could never resist helping someone in need. You can't deny it."

I couldn't.

"Before long, Hannon is going to make this an official part of your job description. *Conservatory Inspector General*. It has a nice ring to it, don't you think?"

I let out a clipped laugh. "That would give me something to talk about at Christmas this year, that's for sure."

"Speaking of Christmas . . . what are your plans?" He stole a glance at me as "There's No Place Like

Home for the Holidays" drifted from the truck's speakers, adding a sense of nostalgia to our conversation.

I frowned at the question. I didn't mean to. I really didn't. But I was dreading the holiday, which was normally one of my favorites.

I wasn't as great at dealing with change as I'd thought I was.

Phil was dead. Scarlett at college. My brother working a security job in Iraq.

What I'd thought was a stable marriage may have been anything but.

I frowned and let out a long breath. "Scarlett said she'd come here to celebrate. But her new boyfriend invited her to go with his family on a Caribbean cruise."

Weston flinched. "A Caribbean cruise or Christmas with her mom? I think the choice is clear."

"Mom, right?"

"Absolutely." He didn't hesitate.

I let out a sigh as I stared out the truck window. "I told Scarlett to do whatever she wanted. She hasn't told me yet what her choice is."

"I hope she chooses wisely."

I fought a frown at the emotional dilemma raging inside me. "I want her to have fun and live her own best life. I don't want to hold her back."

"There's nothing wrong with wanting to spend Christmas with your child." Weston cast me a knowing smile before putting his truck in Park. "We're here."

We climbed out and walked toward Bartholomew's, which was located in a quaint storefront on River Street. Neon-blue letters above the front door led the way, and a fire escape snaked down from six floors above, making the area look even more intriguing.

Weston ordered for us, making banter with Bart and Irma, the owners and his friends, as he did. Several minutes later, we were seated at a table by the window with a perfect view of the Savannah River.

I took a bite of my salted caramel beignet, letting the sweet powdered-sugar coating melt on my lips in a moment of pure food bliss. I'd eat plenty of carrots and mustard later to make up for this.

I glanced up at Weston and saw him watching me, a grin tugging at his lips.

He was clearly enjoying this too much.

Ignoring his stare, I wiped my mouth and cleared my throat. "Before we talk about The Christmas Thing, what are *your* plans for the holidays?"

His smile slipped. "Athena has Allison and Tyler for Christmas."

Athena was his ex-wife, a woman who'd cheated on him and then taken his kids away. The whole situation had been heartbreaking for him—and his children. Divorce almost always was.

"So, I'm not sure," he said. "Part of me is considering going back to Nashville to visit some friends. It would keep my mind off things."

I held back a frown. Weston understood. He knew what it was like to lose people you loved. To have to recalibrate your future. To start over.

Life was messy. People were broken. So broken.

All of us.

Some simply hid it better than others.

That had become more and more apparent as I'd gotten older. The illusion of perfect was just that—an unreachable illusion.

Weston let out a breath as if trying to release himself from burdensome thoughts. "Okay. I guess we should talk about some details for this event."

I sensed he wanted to change the subject, and I was okay with that. "Of course."

Maybe talking about The Christmas Thing would be a good distraction from my otherwise melancholy holiday thoughts.

———

An hour later, Weston and I had worked out the final details for The Christmas Thing.

There was so much talent at the conservatory that we weren't lacking for good entertainment. At the request of the students, Weston and I were emceeing the event. Money from the ticket sales would go to struggling families in the community to help them have a merrier Christmas.

We arrived back at the school, and Weston strolled with me toward my office in the administrative wing. His was located in the education wing two buildings over.

I'd had a nice time with Weston today. I'd always enjoyed being with him . . . until he'd broken my heart.

I frowned.

Ultimately, our breakup had been a blessing in disguise. I'd realized I didn't want to be in the spotlight. I'd met and married Phil. Scarlett had been born.

I often thought about how differently my life would have turned out with Weston. I would have probably stayed on the music scene. Maybe my fame would have grown. It was anyone's guess what that might have led to.

From my experience, probably nothing good. There were very few people I knew who were both famous and happy. The cycle of seeking after more led to a pattern of unhappiness I'd seen over and over again.

We paused by my office door, and Weston turned toward me. Based on the look in his eyes, he had something he wanted to say to me.

I licked my lips as I waited.

"Camryn—" he started.

I was right.

Whatever he needed to tell me, it was serious. His voice was at least two octaves higher than usual.

Before he could finish—or start, really—a boisterous voice sounded from inside my office. "Camryn Paine . . ."

I turned and gasped at the familiar face I saw sitting in a chair by my desk.

"Zeke Bancroft?"

As he stood, I hurried toward him and threw my arms around him.

I couldn't believe this blast from my past was here.

CHAPTER
THREE

AFTER ZEKE SET me back on my feet, I stared at him another moment, feeling my mind drift back in time.

Zeke Bancroft.

The man was six-foot-three and broad, with a square face, short dark hair, and perceptive eyes. The way he held himself showed discipline and hard work. He was nearing fifty but could win any competition against someone twenty years younger.

I glanced back at Weston and realized I was being rude. I stepped away from Zeke and straightened my blouse, which had billowed out from my skirt as I'd reached up to hug Zeke.

"I'm so sorry," I started, hating how flustered I felt. "Weston, this is Zeke Bancroft. Zeke, Weston Turner."

Zeke's eyes glimmered with familiarity as he turned to Weston. "I've heard of you. Love your song 'Rocking Lot of Love.' Played it at my wedding reception."

Weston grinned, though it didn't quite reach his eyes. "That's a fan favorite."

Zeke shifted. "I didn't realize you were teaching here at the school."

Weston nodded, his gaze still appearing apprehensive. "I haven't been here long. I just needed a break from being on the road so much."

The truth was, Weston had come here so he could have a more stable schedule and see his kids more often. The man had practically been on tour for the last twenty years, selling out concert venues and stadiums. Rumor had it that some prospective students had applied here at the conservatory just because Weston was teaching.

Weston stared at me another moment as if waiting for more of an explanation as to Zeke's appearance. Weston didn't know who Zeke was—of course. Where was my head right now?

"Zeke and Phil were business partners," I explained.

Weston nodded slowly as if taking his time comprehending the nature of our relationship. "I see."

"He was the brains, I was the brawn." Zeke grinned. "That's what I always said."

"Marine?" Weston asked.

"How'd you know?"

"I can spot you guys a mile away. There's something different about the way you carry yourself." Weston extended his hand. "Thank you for your service."

Zeke gave him a hearty handshake. "I appreciate that."

Weston stepped back, and his gaze met mine. "I'll let you two talk. We'll catch up later."

Was that disappointment in his gaze? Or was I seeing what I wanted to see?

I was rusty and out of practice when it came to dating. Truthfully, I wasn't sure I wanted to jump back into the scene anytime soon. And, if I did, I wasn't sure I'd want to jump into it with Weston—if that was even what he'd wanted to talk to me about.

But I'd be lying if I said there wasn't something there between us. Nothing official. Nothing we'd spoken about. Just years and years of history and memories.

Being a widow wasn't the path I'd expected my life to take, but I had to make the best of it.

Truthfully, there were things I loved about being on my own.

And there were things I hated.

As Weston disappeared down the hallway, I turned back to Zeke and plastered on a smile. "This is so unexpected. What brings you to Grand Isle?"

A shadow fell over his gaze. "I happened to be in town so I thought maybe we could catch up." He shrugged. "It's been a while."

There was more to this. I knew there was. I heard it in Zeke's voice.

But I wouldn't address that head-on—not yet.

"Yes, it has been a long time," I said instead. "I'm so glad you're here."

He shifted, his gaze still masked and almost mysterious. "Let's grab dinner later."

"That sounds perfect."

He grinned. "Great. How about if I pick you up at seven?"

"I'll be waiting."

I rattled off my address and then he slipped out the door, saying something about a meeting he needed to attend.

When he left, I couldn't help but feel a sense of excitement.

Seeing Zeke was a nice reminder of my past—at least, one version of my past.

Did he have the answers I needed about Phil and Andrea?

Did I dare ask him?

I wasn't sure.

———

As soon as Zeke left and I sat down at my desk, another shadow filled my doorway. My office appeared to be one of the most popular at the school today.

To my surprise, I spotted Barbara Abernathy standing there.

I rushed to my feet and smoothed my pencil skirt. The woman had that effect on people—kind of like royalty did.

"Mrs. Abernathy . . . come in."

"I'm sorry to stop by unannounced like this." She gripped her purse, almost reminding me of a queen surveying her people—her people being me. Again— like royalty.

She stepped inside and closed the door before sitting across the desk from me. I lowered myself back into my chair, curious about why she was here. She didn't seem like the type to stop by for no reason.

"I'd like to hire you," she announced.

I blinked, unsure if I'd heard her correctly. "Hire me for what?"

"To find my missing violin."

At once, something close to panic filled me. "I'm sorry. There must be a misunderstanding. I'm not sure what Skittles told you, but I'm not actually a private investigator."

Her expression remained unchanged. "I know. But your reputation precedes you."

"I have no experience."

"That's okay. I'm an excellent judge of character. I can sense by looking at you that you're the right person for this job."

A million excuses rushed through my mind. The last thing I wanted was to get myself in over my head—and, as a result, to disappoint someone. "I'm afraid I would just be wasting your time."

"I beg to differ. Accept this job offer. I insist, and I won't leave until you do."

I balked. I hadn't expected that . . . "I'm honored. However, I have a full-time job here at Grand Isle."

"I already talked to Joseph. He said he's okay with you accepting this temporary job and even working during school hours."

My eyebrows shot up. Money had an amazing influence on people. Since the Abernathys were major donors to the school, Joseph was clearly making some concessions—and making it hard for me to say no.

I shifted in my seat as I tried to figure out the best

way to handle her offer. "Are you sure this is what you want to do? There are a lot more experienced investigators out there."

"Positive. I'm willing to supply you any information or means you need to look into my missing violin."

I drew in a breath, trying to recalculate my thoughts. Every time I blinked, Mrs. Abernathy was dropping a new surprise bomb on me. The job offer. Joseph. Information and concessions.

I needed to buy some time here. "Let's backtrack and talk about exactly what happened. Can you give me any more information on this violin?"

She slid a piece of paper toward me. "This is what I've got. I've also written down everything I know about this moving company, including the phone number I used to contact them. My video doorbell caught images of several of the workers, so if you give me your email, I can send those to you as well."

"If you could send the entire videos, that would be helpful." I might hear something in the background of one of them that could ultimately help me if I decided to accept her job offer, which I still wasn't sure about.

"And I'll pay you," Mrs. Abernathy added. "Of course."

I wasn't too concerned with money.

Truthfully, I secretly loved the idea of being some type of crime fighter. But I was also realistic, and I knew I wasn't trained. Even if my husband had owned a private security firm, that didn't mean his skills or knowledge had rubbed off on me.

Mrs. Abernathy offered a curt nod as she rose from her seat. "Anything else that you need, let me know. I'll be happy to share with you. I just want that Stradivari back. I know a missing violin probably isn't at the top of the police's to-do list. I have no choice but to take matters into my own hands."

I leaned forward on my desk. "I'll tell you what. I'll see what I can do. I don't want to make any promises I can't keep. I don't want to tell you I can find your violin when I'm not sure I can. But I'll look into what happened and see if I can find out anything. How does that sound?"

A smile spread across her face. "That sounds perfect. I just know that you're not going to let me down."

Something about her words added another layer of pressure on me. And I didn't really like being pressured.

But knowing Joseph, he was banking on the fact that I'd solve this case.

I frowned.

As Mrs. Abernathy walked away, I wondered what exactly I'd just agreed to.

CHAPTER
FOUR

AS SOON AS I heard my doorbell ring that evening, I ran my hand down the charcoal-colored wrap dress I'd decided on for our dinner. I didn't want to look overdone, yet I didn't want to look like I didn't care either.

This outfit was going to have to do—I'd tried on four different dresses before deciding on this one. Besides, it wasn't like I was going on a date with Zeke. Or even anything close to a date.

But I'd be lying if I denied that my heart grew warm when I opened the door and saw Zeke standing there in his dress shirt and tie and wearing a grin on his face.

He looked me up and down with unbridled approval. "You look fantastic, Camryn."

"You don't look bad yourself." I grinned back at

him. "Let me just grab my purse, and I'll be ready to go."

He lingered in the doorway, staring inside my apartment. "Nice place."

I glanced around my new home and shrugged. My six hundred square-foot, second-floor apartment featured a set of patio doors leading out to a wrought-iron balcony. The place had initially charmed me with its interesting angles and nooks.

"I like it here. Since I don't plan on staying in Savannah forever, I got this place already furnished and within walking distance of work."

"Seems perfect then."

With my purse in hand, I stepped toward him. "I'm ready."

After locking the door behind me, we walked beside each other down the steps and outside toward Zeke's black Mercedes SUV in the parking lot. I slipped inside and noted that the interior was immaculate—just as I'd expected.

Zeke was the type who made his bed every morning, who always washed his dishes after using them, and who never had a hair out of place.

He defined self-disciplined.

"I made reservations at a French restaurant downtown," I told him. "I think you're going to like it."

"You know I can never turn down French cuisine."

"I actually did remember that." We'd gone on several double dates together in the past, and I'd always been entertained that a tactical guy like Zeke liked fancy food in dainty restaurants.

We made casual conversation about the city on the short ride to the restaurant. When we arrived, a valet parked Zeke's SUV, and we slipped inside the brick building with ivy creeping up the front.

We were seated right away. The place had small candles on each linen-covered table. Classy pictures of Paris graced the walls, and the scents of freshly baked bread, garlic, and olive oil filled the air.

Despite the upscale surroundings, the place still felt casual enough to relax.

"So how have you been doing?" Zeke stared at me from across the table. "It looks like this move has been good for you."

I thought about my life over the past couple of months before slowly nodding. "Being at Grand Isle has definitely been interesting, and the change of scenery has been nice. I only intended on being here on a temporary basis, but the school has asked me to stay on longer."

"Then they must really like you. Of course, what's there not to like?" He grinned.

My cheeks flushed—the action surprising me. I'd been given plenty of compliments in my life—plenty of insults too.

But I felt like I should be beyond the blushing phase of my life.

"You're too kind," I finally said. "But there's plenty about me not to like."

Zeke gave me a look before tilting his head. "Like what?"

"Like I can be neurotic at times. If you think you're going to whisper something and I'm not going to hear, then you're wrong. I can be an introvert one minute and an extrovert the next, which can really confuse some people. I eat carrots dipped in mustard. Need I go on?"

"Well, if those are your worst qualities, then I still say you're pretty close to perfect."

For some reason, my cheeks heated—again—at his words. I cleared my throat, determined to change the subject before he thought I looked like a blushing schoolgirl. "Tell me about you. What's been going on?"

He leaned back and let out a short breath as if gathering his thoughts. "I've been working hard. Joel keeps me up to date with how you're doing."

My brother had taken over the company for Phil after he passed. So far, the partnership seemed to be doing well, at least from what I had heard. Joel really seemed to love it.

"How's Carlena?" Carlena was the only girlfriend Zeke had had since his divorce.

"We broke up."

My eyes widened. I'd thought for sure the two of them were serious. "I'm sorry to hear that."

"Don't be. It was for the best." His voice didn't hold regret, but maybe sadness instead.

It sounded like the breakup was either mutual or Zeke's idea. I wondered what had happened, but I didn't feel like it was my place to ask. Zeke had always been more of Phil's friend than mine, though the two of us had a good relationship.

The server brought some bread, freshly whipped butter, and carrot amuse bouche—all of which were my favorites.

"I have something interesting to share," I announced. I couldn't get Mrs. Abernathy's offer out of my mind, and Zeke would be the perfect person to talk to about it.

Besides, it was a nice distraction from other thoughts—like Zeke's real reason for being here. I sensed something heavy was coming, and I wanted to put it off for a while longer.

I casually spread some butter on my bread,

unsure how Zeke would react to what I was about to say.

"I can't wait to hear. Let me guess: you have a new man in your life?"

I might have blushed again. "No, no new men in my life."

"Not even Weston Turner?" Zeke tilted his head, giving me a knowing look.

I practically snorted—which might have been overdoing it. "No, Weston and I are just friends. We had our chance together a long time ago, and that proved we weren't meant to be."

"Speaking of a long time ago, I still remember when Phil and I were hired to protect you . . . you know, back when you were a youngster." Zeke's eyes sparkled at his statement.

"A youngster? I was old enough for Phil to ask me out."

"No one was more shocked when you said yes than I was—or maybe Phil."

I smiled. "He was seven years older than me, but I needed that maturity in my life back then."

"And he needed your youthfulness." Zeke smiled softly. "The two of you had a good life together."

I swallowed back what I wanted to say. But those emails I'd found . . . they weren't something I was ready to talk about yet. Making accusations like that . . . it could ruin Phil's legacy. Ruin my memories. Throw Scarlett into a tailspin if she found out.

Subjects like an affair needed to be handled with wisdom.

Instead, I paused with a piece of bread in my hand and forced a smile. "Yes, Phil and I did have a good life together."

"But that's not what you wanted to tell me about."

I let out a long breath, grateful for the subject change. "No, it's not. What I wanted to tell you about is the fact that I've been asked to investigate a theft."

His eyebrows shot up, and he leaned forward with his elbows on the table. "Now *this* I've got to hear."

I ran through the case details with him before asking, "What do you think? Am I crazy if I say yes?"

"I have to agree that your ear for things will be a unique asset to this investigation. And you've always been astute. You helped Phil and me that time we were investigating a missing child. You heard church bells ringing in the background of the ransom call. Remember that?"

"I'll never forget it. I was glad I could help return the child to her parents."

The girl had been the same age as Scarlett at the

time she was abducted. I hadn't been able to sleep as I'd imagined how her parents must have felt.

I pulled off a piece of bread and nibbled on it. "If you were investigating this stolen violin, what would you do first?"

"Definitely watch those videos your client sends you and see if you can pick up on anything. Then check local pawn shops. You said these kinds of moving company scams have been happening throughout Georgia?"

"That's what I've been told."

"Then that means these guys may not have known about the violin and how much it's worth."

"But the instrument wasn't even supposed to be packed, so maybe these guys upped their game."

"You could be right. I'd still check pawn shops, just to be certain. Then, after that, I'd look into local auctions—although if the thief is smart, he'd go outside this area to make the sale."

"What about online auctions?"

"Too risky. They wouldn't want too many people asking questions about it."

I stored that information away as our food was delivered. I'd ordered trout almondine. Zeke had gotten steak au poivre.

After we'd prayed over the food, I knew I needed to get to the heart of the matter and find out why he was really in Savannah. "What brings you out this way, Zeke?"

Suddenly, his expression seemed to turn grim. "You, actually."

I pointed to myself. "Me? I don't understand."

The grim expression on his face only grew even more foreboding. "I've been looking into something, and I wanted to tell you about it face-to-face."

Face-to-face? That didn't sound good.

Was this about Phil and Andrea?

Zeke's shoulders stiffened, and I heard the catch in his voice as he began. "There was a break-in at the office the other day."

"I'm sorry to hear that." I was unsure where Zeke was going with this, but certain that now that he'd started, I couldn't *not* hear. My initial thoughts were incorrect—this wasn't personal, was it?

His serious gaze connected with mine. "I walked into the office and heard this guy talking on the phone with someone. He didn't know I was there, so I listened. Your name was mentioned."

"My name?" My voice inched up a notch.

Zeke nodded, his expression somber. "He said you knew something, and he couldn't let you tell anyone."

"What?" Surprise coursed through me. "What does that mean?"

"I was hoping you could tell me. I tackled the guy, but he put up a good fight. He hit me over the head and had me seeing stars long enough for him to escape."

"I'm so sorry to hear that. Are you okay?"

He nodded and touched the side of his head—probably where he'd been hit. "I'm fine."

My heart pounded harder. "Did you see his face?"

He frowned and his eyes glazed as if reliving the moment. "No. He was wearing a mask. I tried to follow him, but I was too late." He stared at me again. "I'm worried for your safety, Camryn."

I searched my thoughts. "I have no idea why he would have mentioned me. Was there anything else that gave you any clues?"

"As I started going through our filing cabinet, I noticed one of our client's files was missing. It took me a while to figure out which one. It was for a company called Bromtech up in Charleston."

I shrugged. "I've never heard of it."

He dipped his head. "Are you sure? I was hoping you might know why someone would grab that file."

"I have no idea. Can you tell me anything about the case you worked for them?"

"It wasn't anything that notable. We were guarding the CEO—a man named Clive Bromarski—

after he got some threats against him. You ever heard his name?"

"Doesn't ring a bell."

"Bromtech is a government contractor, and Bromarski made some people mad when he merged with another company and cut his work force in half." He stared at me. "Any of that sound familiar?"

I shrugged, wishing I had some insight to offer. My responses were disappointing, to say the least. "It doesn't make any sense. Phil was hands-off on the tactical side of things. You were the one who did the footwork."

"For that case, we had to pull Phil into it. We were short-staffed, and the assignment seemed easy. I mean, Bromarski is a smart guy, but also a desk jockey. He developed a new type of bulletproof armor that he sold to the government, along with some other equipment that he licensed."

I shook my head. "It seems like I would remember Phil mentioning the fact that he was acting as security for someone . . ."

"He was out of town a lot."

I couldn't argue with that. His travels had seemed innocent at the time. But what if it was because Phil was meeting another woman? Meeting Andrea?

I stared at Zeke, trying to read his expression.

"What are you thinking? The missing file is obviously serious enough that you came here."

Zeke pressed his lips together, and I knew I wouldn't like whatever he was about to say.

"I don't know how to say this," Zeke started. "So, I'm just going to put it out there."

"I can handle it." After all I'd been through in life, I wasn't going to shy away from the truth.

His gaze locked with mine. "I'm worried that Phil got himself involved in something that may have gotten him killed."

CHAPTER
FIVE

I SHOOK my head as Zeke's words sank in. The car accident where he'd died had haunted me ever since.

I still went to therapy as I tried to deal with the loss—and my role in it.

"That's not possible," I rushed. "I was driving when Phil died—"

Zeke's hand clamped down on my arm. "I think the crash was supposed to look like an accident."

I shook my head again, still not believing what I was hearing with my own ears. But I let Zeke continue. I needed to know what else he had to say.

"I think someone wanted Phil dead but needed to cover up that fact. I think the driver of that car set out to hit you guys. The fact that you survived was probably just a coincidence." He paused and pressed his lips together in a frown. "I'm sorry, Camryn."

I wiped beneath my eyes as I felt the moisture there. I hadn't even realized that tears had filled my gaze.

"Is that a theory? Or do you have evidence?" I finally asked.

"I talked to the medical examiner. He said he always thought there was something suspicious about Phil's death. The driver's level of intoxication . . . it wasn't high enough to merit what happened. There were no skid marks. No other cars coming. It was almost like this guy was waiting for you and intended on using his car as a weapon . . ."

A cry escaped from me at his words.

Zeke's hand slid from my arm and covered my hand. "I know this has to be hard to hear."

I tried to focus on facts instead of letting my emotions carry me away. I couldn't let that happen. Not here.

I preferred my grief to be private.

A few deep breaths later, I glanced back up at Zeke. "This guy who broke into the office . . . he said my name to someone on the phone?"

"That's right. Any idea why he thinks you know something?"

"No . . . I have no clue at all." I shrugged, desperation for answers trying to strangle me. All I knew was that I wanted to crumble inside, to completely fall apart. But that wasn't an option. "Why do you think Phil was killed?"

"The Bromtech case . . . it was a month before he died. I remember Phil seemed distracted, like something was on his mind, but he wouldn't tell me what."

A month before he died . . . that was around the same time of those emails with Andrea. Had that relationship distracted him?

No, that wouldn't make sense. An affair wouldn't have gotten him killed.

I'd looked into the woman. She was an accountant. Single. Beautiful.

"That's why you came here? You think I might really know something." My throat burned as I waited for Zeke's response.

"I came here because I'm worried about you. Plus, Charleston isn't far from here, so I'm heading there on Tuesday to do some investigating."

I swallowed hard. "I see."

"What can I do for you, Camryn?"

That was an excellent question.

"I have no idea." Another thought hit me, and my gaze snapped to Zeke's. "Does Joel know about this?"

Zeke shook his head. "I came to you first. I thought that was only fair."

Good. I needed to keep this quiet for a while longer—especially for Scarlett's sake. She'd been devastated when her father died. I didn't want to pile any more emotional baggage on her.

"Everyone loved Phil," I finally said. "I can't imagine anyone wanting to hurt him."

Phil had been the consummate businessman. He knew how to read people, how to make them feel special—and it wasn't because he was being fake. He was just so good at working with people, and that amazing quality had gotten him far in the business world.

The security firm wasn't his only business. He'd started several others before, either selling them or taking a hands-off leadership role.

"I agree," Zeke said. "Phil was one of the most likable guys I've ever met. But that doesn't mean he didn't have enemies, especially considering our line of work. He could've stumbled into something."

"Oh, Zeke . . ." I pushed my plate away. I wasn't sure I'd be able to eat now.

What if Phil had been murdered?

That question replaced my earlier question: what if Phil was having an affair?

"I'm sorry, Camryn." Zeke's apologetic eyes met mine. "I didn't want to upset you."

"I'm glad you came to me. I . . ." I shook my head,

unsure what exactly I should say right now. "I just don't know what to think."

"Once the shock wears off, I have a few questions for you."

A few questions? I had more than a few.

I nodded, wondering when this numbness would dissipate. "Of course. Whatever you need."

———

"You still don't drive?" Zeke asked as we headed back to my apartment.

"I don't." My heart seemed to lodge in my throat at his question. "I just can't seem to bring myself to get back behind the wheel."

Guilt had plagued me for years. Along with PTSD. Replays of the sound of tires burning against the asphalt. Soundbites of the crunching of metal. Of the silence that had followed. Of hearing Phil suck in his last breaths while I watched helplessly.

"It's understandable after what you went through," Zeke said. "I think the first time will be the hardest. Each time afterward will get a little easier."

"You think?"

"I do. I remember walking into the middle of an ambush on one mission in Iraq. We were all lucky to get out of it alive. Every time we had a similar mission after that, I'd get so much anxiety that I wasn't sure I'd be able to do my job. But one way or another, I made it through."

"I can only imagine."

I still felt numb as Zeke walked me up to my apartment. I paused at the door, wondering if I should invite him in so we could talk more. Another part of me wanted to be alone so I could process what I'd learned.

"Do you mind if I come in for a second?" he asked.

I guess that settled my mental debate. "Of course not. Come on in."

"I want to make sure everything is okay before I leave—just in case someone is targeting you."

"Someone from Bromtech?"

He shrugged. "Not necessarily. There's still a lot we don't know. I need to figure out who exactly was threatening Bromarski. I have a meeting with him Tuesday."

I still didn't move. "You really think I could be in danger? I don't know anything. Phil is dead. What would that prove?"

Zeke's eyes looked stormy as his gaze connected with mine. "According to what I overheard these guys think you know something."

I brushed off his words with a quick, airy laugh. We were overreacting. That was all there was to it.

"This is all ridiculous," I muttered, halfway trying to convince myself as I unlocked and opened the door.

But just as I said the words, I glanced into my apartment.

My window was cracked open. My breath caught at the sight of it.

"Camryn?"

I pointed to the window. "Zeke, I didn't leave my apartment like that."

CHAPTER
SIX

"STAY BACK." Zeke seemed to sense my distress.

And I wasn't going to argue with him.

I scooted against the wall and held my breath as I waited to see what he might discover.

Had someone been in my apartment?

That's how it appeared.

A few minutes later, Zeke returned and shoved his gun back into its holster. "Everything's clear. I'd like for you to look around and make sure nothing is missing or out of place."

I must have sent him a terrified look because he added, "I'll stay with you as you do."

That sounded perfect.

I made my way around the apartment, looking for anything that might give me a clue as to what someone had been doing inside my place.

But I saw nothing unusual. If it wasn't for the window being open, I would have never known.

I paused in the kitchen and turned back toward Zeke, my safe haven suddenly not feeling as safe.

"Are you certain you didn't leave that window cracked?" Zeke's gaze locked with mine.

I nodded. "I'm a single woman living by myself. I keep my windows locked."

"I don't like this." His jaw set in a firm line. "I'd hoped whoever was behind this wouldn't act so soon."

I tried to think through various scenarios, but there were too many possibilities to make sense of this. "Do you think this guy who broke into the security office followed you here?"

Zeke's jaw seemed to tighten even more. "That's nearly impossible to say. I don't want to think that's true. But it could be."

"Or what if this open window has something to do with the missing violin?"

His gaze narrowed as he studied me a moment. "Why would someone break in because of that? You've barely started to investigate."

I shrugged. He had a point. "I did go to the crime scene where the dead body was found. But you're right. I've made zero headway. I really don't know what to think. I just feel uneasy, to say the least."

Zeke frowned as he glanced around my apartment again. "I'm liking this less and less all the time."

A shiver rushed down my spine. "You're not the only one."

Someone had been inside my private space.

It seemed as if I may have gotten myself wrapped up in not *one* but *two* possible crimes.

That meant I most likely wouldn't be getting any sleep tonight.

———

I took a sip of my coffee, still trying to compose myself. Normally, I didn't have caffeine this late. But, tonight, caffeine seemed to offer some kind of strange comfort. Zeke had agreed and was sipping on a cup also.

As we sat there, my phone buzzed. It was Mrs. Abernathy.

My pulse quickened when I saw she'd sent me the doorbell videos of the movers.

"What is it?" Zeke leaned closer.

"It's footage of the people who stole that violin." I hit Play, and Zeke leaned even closer as we watched the video together. A clean, minty scent filled my nostrils—a scent that I found very nice.

I pushed those thoughts aside. There was no way I was attracted to my husband's best friend. That would just be weird.

The video started with two men carrying a couch out the front door.

"Pause it there," Zeke said.

I did as he asked and studied the images on the screen. I squinted, trying to get a better look at the two men pictured. They both wore baseball caps pulled low over their eyes, so it was hard to get a good look at their faces.

They appeared to be in their early thirties, if I had to guess. Both wore oversized sweatshirts and jeans, which only further added to their ambiguity.

"Maybe these images will give the police something to go on," Zeke said. "I'm not sure how much help the video will be to us, though. Play some more."

I pressed Play and watched as the two men continued to carry the couch to a moving truck parked in the driveway. A moment later, a third man carried out a box.

My breath caught when I saw him.

This was the dead man.

The one from the alley.

Why had he died? What had happened to put him on the outs with the other two guys?

I had a hard time believing some random person had killed him. His death was connected with this scheme they had going on.

What if this guy had a change of heart and threatened to turn the other two in? What if he went against their original plan and tried to strong-arm the other two into doing something they didn't want to do?

As their voices sounded through the video, I noted that one of them had a Boston accent. I closed my eyes as I memorized the sound of his voice.

That could help me later.

"Promise me one thing," Zeke said as he turned to me.

"What's that?"

"Phil would never forgive me if I let you just walk into this blindly. You have to be careful. Anytime that you think you might be in danger, I need you to call me. Please."

"The problem with danger is you don't always know when it's going to appear." I had firsthand experience with that.

His lips flickered down in a frown. "I understand. But if you ever go to question someone or to investigate something—something that involves more than making a phone call or researching something on the computer—please let me know."

I studied his face a moment as I weighed my options. "How long do you plan on being in town?"

His gaze locked with mine. "For as long as necessary."

CHAPTER
SEVEN

"THE POLICE JUST CALLED," Mrs. Abernathy announced.

I blinked as I sat in my office the next afternoon. I'd gone to church and eaten a salad at my house before coming into work.

I usually didn't come in on Sundays, but I still had a lot to do. I'd have a chance to relax next week when I was on break.

I turned my attention back to my phone call. Mrs. Abernathy had said the police had called her . . . this could be interesting.

"Is that right?" I asked.

"They identified the dead man. Detective Garrison only told me because he needed to know if I recognized the name. Arnold Myers."

I stored away that information. "Did you recognize the name?"

"No, I've never heard of him. But Garrison also said that Arnold is a mechanic at Blue's Garage downtown. Or, should I say, he was."

I made another mental note. "Thanks for sharing."

"Any updates?" Mrs. Abernathy's voice contained a hopeful lilt.

"Not yet. But I'm only just getting started." I'd decided I was going to do this. I was going to see what exactly I could find out about this stolen Stradivari. Investigating would be a nice distraction from my other troubles if nothing else.

"Please, let me know the moment you find out anything."

As I ended the call, I realized I needed to head to Blue's Garage and talk to Arnold Myers' coworkers. I needed to find out all I could about the man if I wanted to proceed.

But I'd promised Zeke I wouldn't do anything like that alone.

Why had I promised that again?

Oh, yeah. Because he'd brought up Phil. How could I say no?

Besides, Zeke was right. I wasn't trained to defend myself. If I found myself in the wrong place at the wrong time, my daughter could end up without a father *and* mother. I couldn't do that to Scarlett—not if I could help it.

Zeke had told me that all I had to do was call him. But that made me feel like such a bother . . .

"Who was that handsome chunk of meat with you last night?" Skittles swung around the doorway and into my office, a handful of yellow candy in her hands.

I nearly jumped out of my office chair at her sudden appearance.

My hand rushed over my heart. "Skittles . . ."

"Sorry—didn't mean to scare you. I figured you heard me coming." She popped a piece of candy in her mouth. "You usually do."

I noted she was eating only yellow today. Yellow meant she was happy.

Yes, she determined her treat colors based on her mood—just one of the many interesting things about her.

"I should have, but I was distracted."

"Distracted with thoughts of that handsome chunk of meat?"

I tilted my head. "You mean Zeke?"

"Call him whatever you want." She wagged her eyebrows.

"He's more than a chunk of meat. He's a decorated Marine who's selflessly put his life on the line for others."

She sat across from me, her eyes sparkling. "That's even better."

I gave her another look. Then I realized I wasn't getting rid of her and sighed. "If you must know, Zeke was my husband's best friend and business partner."

"Is he single? I mean, he's too old for me. But not for you . . ." She stared at me, that glimmer still in her eyes.

"He is single, but I'm not looking for romance. I think I told you that before."

"I was totally rooting for you and Weston. But maybe now I'm changing my mind . . ."

"Very funny." I needed to change the subject. Pronto. "Can I help you with something?"

"I just thought you'd like to know that Professor Amile is one of the leading experts on 'fine and rare musical instruments.'" She said this with a fake Italian accent as if that would make him seem even more qualified. "It's a pretty well-known fact around here, but I wasn't sure you'd been here long enough to know."

I blinked, uncertain if I'd heard her correctly. "What?"

"It's true. People interview him all the time for

articles. I heard Art Recovery International has even sought out his help."

I nodded slowly as I processed that helpful little tidbit. "That's . . . very useful. Thank you."

Skittles grinned. "No problem. And, just in case you're wondering, he's at work today. I already checked."

———

Thirty minutes later, I knocked on Professor Amile's door. I didn't know for sure that he'd still be here, but I thought I'd take the chance that he was.

I was in luck.

From the small window on the side of his door. I saw him sitting behind his desk.

I'd met the man a couple of times before, but he wasn't particularly friendly. Lukas Amile was in his seventies, with white hair, a black-and-white-peppered beard, and black glasses with circular frames—very color-coordinated, if you asked me.

He gave off a reclusive, standoffish vibe, to say the least.

As if to confirm that, when I knocked on his door, he glanced up and glared as if he didn't appreciate the interruption.

"Can I help you?" His words sounded crisp and pointed.

I opened his door and stuck my head inside. "I'm hoping you might be able to. I'm Camryn Paine. I'm the Chief Communications Officer here at the school. I have a question for you."

He narrowed his eyes. "I gathered that. What can I do for you?"

The man didn't have a British accent . . . or did he? It seemed like a weird question to ask myself, especially since I was currently listening to him speak. But his words sounded pompous and gave the impression that he thought highly of himself.

I took a step into his office. "I'm helping a family whose valuable antique violin was stolen. I heard that you might have some insight on that."

"Some insight on stealing violins?" He pressed his lips together as if I were an unintelligent ignoramus.

"No, of course not. But on the violin—" I stopped myself when I saw the twinkle in his eyes.

He'd been joking with me. Who would have thought?

Amile shifted, looking overly pleased with himself. "What do you need to know?"

I let out my breath, wondering why I felt so

nervous. Then I dove into my story about what had happened with the Abernathys.

"I'm very familiar with that violin," he finished. "I'm surprised that the FBI's Art Crime Team hasn't gotten involved yet."

"Maybe they will. The instrument just went missing yesterday. I'm not sure how these things work. Is there a black market for musical instruments?"

He leaned back in his seat. "Not usually. In my experience, whenever an instrument of this caliber goes missing it's a crime of opportunity. A thief simply sees the instrument and grabs it, thinking that maybe they can make a few hundred off it."

"If they don't know how valuable it is, then it seems likely that they might just take it to a pawn shop or something."

"Again, in my experience, that's usually what happens."

"Very interesting," I muttered. "I guess I could call around to some pawn shops and see if anyone's been looking to sell a violin."

"Good luck with that." The skeptical look in his eyes clearly said that he didn't think I would be successful.

I knew finding this instrument was going to be

tricky, but when people didn't believe in me, their doubt only made me want to try harder.

Challenge accepted.

"Thanks for your help." No need to burn any bridges. I might need this guy's expertise again sometime in the future, so I needed to play nice.

I glanced at my watch. Zeke was going to pick me up in an hour.

Yes, I'd called him before talking to Amile.

I knew I needed to go to Blue's Garage, and I was trying to be a good girl and stick to my word.

In the meantime, I had a few things to do back in my office . . . including working on another press release for the upcoming Christmas extravaganza.

CHAPTER
EIGHT

"ANYTHING else suspicious happen to you since last night?" Zeke asked as we walked down the sidewalk.

Even though it was December, the day outside was temperate, and it felt good to stretch my legs. Blue's Garage was only a few blocks from the campus, so traveling on foot seemed like a good idea. Plus, Zeke was up for the stroll.

"No, nothing else suspicious," I answered.

"That's good."

"Have you made any headway on your investigation into what happened with Phil?" I knew it was a long shot. It hadn't even been twenty-four hours. But I figured it was something to talk about.

"No, not yet. I'm still looking into things." As

Zeke said the words, he scanned everything around us as if looking for trouble.

Seeing him do that made me also look around. Could someone be watching us right now? The person who had killed Phil? Or maybe the person who had stolen the violin and had killed Arnold?

There were so many unknowns right now.

A few minutes later we stopped in front of Blue's Garage. The outside of the building looked neat and tidy. Judging by the cars filling the parking lot, the place had plenty of business coming their way.

As we approached the door, I sucked in a breath and glanced at Zeke. "I guess I should take the lead here?"

He grinned. "This is your investigation."

Yes, it was.

I sucked in one more breath before stepping inside.

I could either be brilliant right now . . . or make a total fool of myself.

———

"Yeah, I was real sorry to hear what happened to Arnold," a man wearing a mechanic's uniform with the name "Carl" stitched across the front said.

He continued to change a set of tires as Zeke and I

stood in the garage, asking him questions. The car shop was bustling with three cars in the bays and a couple out back—including one with a revving engine that set my nerves on edge. Country music— one of Weston's songs, actually—blared from a small speaker set up somewhere nearby.

I tried to tune out all the noises around me so I could concentrate. Sometimes, it was harder than others.

This was one of those times.

Plus, the overwhelming scent of motor oil and exhaust nearly took my breath away.

I was definitely on sensory overload.

"Were you close to Arnold?" I asked.

"Not particularly." Carl tightened some lug nuts, barely making eye contact as he continued to work.

"Did he seem to be distracted before he was killed?" I continued. "Like something was bothering him?"

"I wouldn't know. Arnold quit about two weeks ago."

I exchanged a look with Zeke. Interesting . . .

"Did he say why?" I asked.

"He said he'd found another job." Carl twisted the wrench and let out a grunt. "He didn't say what it was—only that it would be a pay raise."

Could Arnold have found another job—stealing

other people's possessions? That's what it sounded like to me.

"Was he single?" Zeke asked.

"Nah, he had a girlfriend. Mariah, I think was her name."

A girlfriend might have some answers . . . "Do you know where we might find Mariah?"

"Sure, she's a barista at the shop the next block over. At least, she was last time I talked to Arnold."

I stored that information away. This conversation hadn't led me to any definitive answers, but a better picture of Arnold had formed in my mind.

That was useful in itself.

In theory, at least.

As Zeke and I left the garage, I nearly collided with someone.

I looked up and spotted Detective Garrison staring at me.

"How did you know to come here?" he demanded.

I shrugged. "I have my ways."

He cast me another skeptical glance. "I suppose you do."

With a dirty look, he strode past me and into the garage.

CHAPTER
NINE

AS SOON AS I walked into The Family Bean, I spotted a woman behind the counter whose name tag clearly read "Mariah."

Jackpot.

She was in her early twenties with blonde hair sporting faded purple and blue streaks. Her face was pale, and she wore no makeup to conceal the dark circles beneath her eyes. The skin around her nose ring appeared red, and tattoos crept from beneath her shirt like vines that couldn't be controlled.

The coffeehouse wasn't busy, so I hoped she might talk to me.

With Zeke at my side, I ordered a vanilla latte, and he asked for a plain black coffee.

As we waited for our drinks, I dove right in with my inquiries. "Listen, I have a question for you."

"Question about coffee?" Mariah stuck a stainless steel cup under the frother and glanced at me, looking almost annoyed—even as the scent of coffee, vanilla, and cinnamon surrounded her.

They were happy scents—to me, at least.

"My name is Camryn Paine, and I actually have a question about Arnold Myers."

She froze a moment, and her gaze fluttered toward mine. "Did you know Arnold?"

"No, I didn't. I'm investigating his death." I shook my head. "Actually, not so much his death but what happened leading up to his death."

She shrugged, a shadow falling over her gaze. The whites of her eyes seemed to turn pink in one watery blink.

"I don't know how I can help you," she muttered. "We broke up a couple of weeks ago."

"First of all, I'm sorry for your loss. And, second, do you mind if I ask why?"

She shrugged, her eyes still wet and distant. "We just weren't working out. Arnold seemed preoccupied and melancholy lately. I'd had enough. He wasn't opening up about what was going on, and I didn't really see how we were going to move forward if there were secrets between us. Secrets only cause division—in my experience, at least."

I followed her down the dessert case as she

continued fixing my drink. "Do you have any idea what happened to cause the change in him?"

"He wouldn't tell me. That was part of our problem." Her eyes narrowed.

"Did you notice any other changes in his behavior? Anything that gave you a clue as to what might be going on?"

She let out an exasperated breath. "At first, I thought he met someone new. I went to surprise him after work one night to see if he might be meeting up with a woman—but he was the one who surprised me. I spotted him talking to these two guys on the street corner. He didn't know I was there."

"What did you do?" I asked.

"I was going to strike up a conversation like it wasn't a big deal. Then I heard their voices. They sounded mad, so I backed off. I didn't want any part of that."

"Was that before or after he quit his job?" I asked.

Mariah hesitated before answering. "I think it was a couple of days before."

"Did you ever ask Arnold about it?" Zeke inserted himself. "Did he tell you what happened?"

"At that point, I knew better than to ask. I figured Arnold wouldn't tell me the truth anyway. But those guys looked like trouble. That's when I knew for sure that I wanted out. I don't need any trouble in my life—especially any troubles from a man."

Could those two guys Arnold was speaking with be the same ones involved in the moving scheme? The assumption seemed like a logical one.

"That just happened two weeks ago?" I clarified.

Mariah thought about it a moment before nodding. "Yes, that's right."

"Could you describe those men?" Zeke's demeanor suddenly turned serious, almost intimidating.

I wasn't certain if he meant to seem tough or if it just came naturally. I was interested in seeing how Mariah would react.

"Like I said, it was dark outside. They were both wearing hats and coats. I wouldn't recognize them if they came in here and ordered coffee, to be honest." She seemed unfazed as if she'd accepted that she'd never know for certain who these guys were.

Disappointment filled me. Then again, I hadn't expected her to have all the answers.

Before I could ask more questions, she handed me my latte and Zeke his coffee. As she did, a group of six customers flooded inside the place.

"I'd love to talk more—not really." Mariah rolled her eyes. "But I've got to get back to work."

Clearly, she was done with this conversation.

I only wished I was able to walk away with something more—more direction as to where to search next in order to find answers.

———

"Maybe you are a natural at investigating. Great job back there."

I stole a side glance at Zeke as we strolled down the sidewalk, sipping warm coffee as we did. "I don't know how natural it is. But I hate unanswered questions. I guess that applies to my life and understanding other people's lives as well."

"I suppose that makes sense."

"I did call around to some pawn shops in the area today, but no one knew anything." I'd done that when I was supposed to be writing a press release. "I was thinking about trying to find some of the other families who were scammed and talking to them, trying to find similarities or new details about these guys."

"That's a great idea."

I was almost certain Zeke had already had the same idea but was trying not to overstep, which I appreciated. But I could still use some pointers.

"How do I track down those other families?" I asked.

"These thefts haven't been widely reported on the news, so I doubt there are any articles out there on it. Though there could be. You might want to do a quick check of social media or even speak with the family who was ripped off. They might know of someone else. I doubt the police will share that information with you. If you get creative enough, you might be able to figure something out."

"I'll see what I can do." Maybe I could ask Detective Garrison.

Then again, I didn't want to put him on the spot. If I called in a favor, it needed to be important because he wasn't going to give out many.

Zeke and I paused outside the school, and I glanced up at him. "What are you going to do now?"

"I'm doing more research on Bromtech and calling the two other guys who worked that case with Phil."

I wondered if he knew more details than he was letting on. That was my guess. But I wouldn't push him—not yet. I trusted his judgment.

Instead, I said, "Thank you for going with me today."

"It's no problem." Zeke didn't step away yet. Instead, he met my gaze with a hopeful look in his eyes. "Can I convince you to go get dessert with me this evening?"

"Dessert sounds fantastic."

I thought about mentioning the beignet place. But something about Bartholomew's seemed special, like it was mine and Weston's spot and not a place to bring other people. I could figure something else out.

"I'll see you later then," I added.

Zeke's grin tugged up a little higher, almost into an all-out smile. "I look forward to it."

CHAPTER
TEN

I GOT BACK in time to meet Weston.

We were going along with a video crew to interview some families we'd be helping through our Christmas fundraiser. In between acts, we'd show snippets of their stories on a screen on the stage.

I hoped this more personal side of the fundraiser would help to bring in more money and make this more meaningful for the students.

Weston agreed to drive, and we were snug in his truck right now with some friendly country tunes crooning through the speakers.

"So, that was quite the surprise that Phil's friend showed up, huh?" Weston said the words casually as he stared at the traffic ahead.

I had a feeling Weston had been dying to ask me

about Zeke's sudden appearance. I was actually surprised it had taken him this long.

"It's been a long time since I've seen Zeke." I forced my voice not to sound melancholy. "I definitely wasn't expecting him to show up."

Nor had I expected him to tell me Phil might have actually been murdered.

"Did he just come so the two of you could catch up?" Weston still looked casual with his hands draped over the steering wheel.

I could be wrong, but I almost thought I noticed a hint of jealousy in his voice. "Unfortunately, I wish that's all there was to it. But nothing in my life is ever that simple now, is it?"

Weston stole a side glance at me. "What's going on?"

I let out a long breath as I tried to figure out exactly how much I wanted to say. Finally, I realized there was no reason not to share this information. In fact, maybe it would feel good to get it off my chest.

"Zeke caught someone breaking into the office of the security company. He . . ." I let out a long breath, unsure if I could finish. I swallowed hard, determined to pull through this. "He now wonders if Phil's death was really an accident."

"What?" Outrage captured Weston's voice as he

tapped on the brakes and looked at me. He quickly righted himself and focused on the road again.

I nodded slowly, still trying to process all this myself. "I know. That's what I said too. I couldn't believe it. I'm still not sure I believe it."

"Did he say what kind of evidence has come forward to make him think that? It's a pretty big claim."

I released another long breath. "He did share a few things."

"Why did he come all the way here to tell you? He's based in Atlanta, right?"

I swallowed hard. "He believes I might be in danger now also."

Saying those words felt surreal.

He tapped the brakes again. "Why would someone want to hurt you? It's been a long time since Phil's death. Wouldn't they have tried to get to you sooner?"

"I wish I knew the answer to that."

"Camryn . . ."

I shrugged as I glanced out the window, trying not to show Weston how upset I really felt. "I know. I'm still trying to process all this."

"I know you've felt guilty since the accident. But if someone did it on purpose . . ."

"It might clear my guilt to know it wasn't my

fault, but I'm not sure it's going to make me feel any better." My words sounded lackluster.

I'd already thought it through. There was no comfort for me in this situation—whatever the outcome.

Weston squeezed my hand. "I'm sorry. I don't know what else to say."

"There really isn't anything else *to* say."

A few minutes of silence passed until finally Weston quietly asked, "How long does Zeke plan on staying?"

"Well, since someone broke into my apartment last night—"

"Wait. Someone broke into your apartment?"

I explained the open window to him. A lot had happened since we'd chatted yesterday.

"I don't like the sound of that." Weston's jaw visibly tightened.

"I don't either. But Zeke said he's going to stay close until he can figure out what exactly is going on."

"Are you sure this doesn't tie in with this new case that you're working?"

"I'm not sure about anything right now."

"Well, if there's anything I can do, would you let me know?"

I nodded. "I'll do that. And thank you so much for listening. I appreciate it."

Just as I said those words, we pulled into the neighborhood where we were meeting one of the families.

As I looked around, I realized this wasn't the best area of town. I didn't anticipate having any trouble here. But I hoped that assumption was correct.

Nothing felt certain right now.

———

"I have to admit that I was expecting something a little fancier." Zeke licked his peppermint ice cream cone as we strolled down River Street.

"I figured you can't go wrong with ice cream."

"Especially not in the winter." Zeke threw me a smile.

"That is an excellent point. But this ice cream is my favorite." I held up my own gingerbread ice cream cone.

"It's all good. I bundled up, so I'll be fine. This actually reminds me of the time you, Phil, Carlena, and I went out on that double date. We ended up drinking hot chocolate even though it was ninety degrees outside."

I laughed at the memory. "It seemed like a good idea at the time."

We paused near the railing and looked over the river as we enjoyed our cones. On the corner, a boy in his late teens played a beat-up violin, his case open in front of him for donations.

"God Rest Ye Merry Gentlemen" rang through the air.

He was good enough to get into the conservatory. But Grand Isle wasn't for everyone. Some people just liked music for the fun of it.

I loved everything about the atmosphere of this moment—the briny scent of the river, the music, the history-steeped buildings.

If only I didn't have so many other worries bogging me down.

"So, anything new?" Zeke stole a glance at me.

"Not really. Work kept me busy for the rest of the day."

"Which work—your actual job or your side gig?"

I smiled. "Both."

"Maybe God is trying to tell you something. Maybe He's saying you went into the wrong line of work." He gave me a pointed look.

"You never know, I suppose. But investigating was always Phil's thing." I took another lick of my gingerbread ice cream. "So, if you don't mind me asking, what happened between you and Carlena?"

Zeke's gaze darkened. "It's a long story."

"I'm sorry." I instantly regretted asking the question. "It's not my business. I just thought for sure that the two of you would get married."

"She wanted me to give up my career. I didn't want to. I figured maybe that was a sign we shouldn't be together."

"I guess the good thing is that you realized the conflict before you got married instead of after."

"That's what I like to tell myself. But I'd known for a while we weren't supposed to be together. I just tried to convince myself that wasn't true."

His words caused a strange sadness to fall over me. "I understand. How long did you date her?"

"Five years."

"That's a long time."

"It is." His voice caught as if this were a hard topic for him. "So, you really haven't dated since Phil passed?"

I shook my head, noting that he'd changed the subject but not making a big deal out of it. If he didn't want to talk more about Carlena, I wouldn't push the subject.

"I mean, I guess I've been out on a few dates. But

they never went anywhere. Sometimes I'm just not sure if I even want to go that route."

"You always have been independent."

I shrugged. "For years, my whole life was about Phil and Scarlett. I did go back to school and get a degree so I could work PR. But . . . I don't know. This feels like the first chance I've had in twenty years to figure out what I really want to do."

"Like publicity?"

"Like publicity . . . or solving crimes." I shrugged again.

He let out a chuckle. "Maybe you could go back to singing."

I tossed the rest of my cone into a nearby trashcan. "No, singing isn't for me anymore. It's not the kind of life I want."

"It's good that you know what you don't want. I can't say the same about my work."

"That's because you feel passionate about what you do. There's nothing wrong with that."

He smiled before turning back toward the river. The moonlight glimmered on his hair as a riverboat paddled by.

This whole town . . . it was atmospheric and wonderful in so many ways.

"I knew I always liked you," Zeke murmured.

"You have a way of reminding me that everything is going to be okay."

"That's because usually everything is going to be okay, one way or another."

Just then, Zeke's face tightened as he looked beyond me. The next instant, he pulled me toward him.

Fear rushed through me, and I glanced over my shoulder. "What is it?"

"I think someone is watching us."

At his words, my muscles went rigid.

"I NEED to get you back to my SUV," Zeke muttered. "Just to be on the safe side."

I glanced around, wondering what—or who—he saw that I didn't. "You think the person watching us is connected to the guy who broke into your office?"

He gripped my arm. "I don't know for sure. But we can't take any chances."

He tossed the rest of his cone into the trash also and tugged me away, acting very much like a bodyguard and reminding me of bygone days. His body shielded mine as he ushered me away from any potential danger.

Suddenly, the streets that just moments earlier I'd been mentally raving over now felt dark and spooky. Nothing seemed safe.

As Zeke escorted me down the sidewalk, footsteps echoed behind us.

My muscles tensed with anticipation.

"Faster," Zeke urged.

He'd heard the footsteps too, hadn't he?

I sensed him moving, reaching for something beneath his jacket.

I knew without looking that it was a gun.

My heart beat even more quickly.

I had no idea what would happen next.

Would the person behind us strike? Or was this guy just trying to intimidate us?

If these were the same people who'd gone after Phil, then I knew that nothing would stand in the way of getting what they wanted—whatever that was.

I would just be a casualty to them.

But I needed some answers as to what was going on here soon.

It appeared that my life depended on knowing the truth.

CHAPTER
TWELVE

AS THE FOOTSTEPS quickened behind us, Zeke pulled me behind a car parked on the side of the street. "Get down!"

I ducked just as he told me. But when I looked up and saw his gun was raised, my head swirled.

What was going on?

"Stay here!" he ordered.

Zeke darted after the man following us.

My breath caught.

What if Zeke got hurt? Or died? Or—

I stopped my worrisome thoughts. They weren't helping me right now.

Instead, I stayed where I was, just as I'd promised.

But my heart thumped in my ears as I waited for whatever would happen next.

I heard footsteps running away. Heard cars in the distance. Heard people walking together.

Please, Lord . . . protect him.

A moment later, more steps walked toward me.

Was it Zeke?

Or was it the person following us?

I braced myself for whatever the outcome.

As a shadow fell over me, I looked up and saw . . .

Zeke.

I released my breath.

He was here.

And he was okay.

Relief swept over me.

"Did you catch him?" I rushed.

He frowned and shook his head, his gaze still scanning everything around us. "Unfortunately, no. He hopped in a car and sped away. He was too far away for me to get a license plate."

I frowned also. "I'm sorry to hear that."

He glanced around again before taking my arm and pulling me to my feet. "We should get you out of here."

I didn't argue about that, especially when I noticed how badly my hands and arms were trembling.

———

We made it back to Zeke's SUV without incident.

But I didn't breathe easier until we arrived back at my apartment. Just like last night, Zeke offered to walk me up, and I didn't refuse.

Part of me feared what I might find once inside. Had someone invaded my space again? And if so, were they looking for something? Or were they just trying to make a point?

Either way, I'd let Zeke check it out first.

I waited outside the door as he searched inside. A moment later, he appeared with a nod and ushered me inside. "Everything's clear. But how would you feel about me sleeping on your couch tonight?"

My breath caught. "You think I'm not safe here with the doors locked?"

"Locks can be picked. I know someone was following us tonight. I don't know what they want, but I have a feeling they know where you live. I don't want to take any chances. Phil would want me to look out for you."

I swallowed a frown.

Was Phil even the person I'd thought he was? Should I mention my suspicions about my husband's unfaithfulness to Zeke? Did I want to know the truth?

I shoved those thoughts aside and turned back to

Zeke. "You're welcome to stay on the couch. It's not very comfortable but . . ."

"I'll be fine. I'm sure I've slept on worse. I *was* a marine."

"Then let me grab some extra sheets, a blanket, and a pillow."

I shouldn't feel as self-conscious as I did while I went to get the items he needed. I wasn't even sure why I felt that way. But my cheeks were warm, and my heartbeat was faster than usual.

A few minutes later, Zeke helped me stretch the sheets over the couch and spread out the blanket, and I tossed the pillow on the other end.

Finally, I turned to him. "What else can I get for you?"

Before he could answer, a knock sounded at the door.

My entire body tensed.

Who would be coming over to my house at this hour?

But when I glanced at the time, I realized it was only nine p.m. It wasn't as late as it felt.

"Stay there." Zeke drew his gun as he strode toward the door.

I lingered behind the wall, keeping one eye on everything just in case.

As he looked through the peephole, his shoulders

relaxed. A moment later, he tucked his gun away and opened the door.

Weston stood there.

His eyes widened when he saw Zeke. "I didn't mean to interrupt anything."

My cheeks heated even more as I stepped toward him. "You're not interrupting anything. Come on in."

"Really, I can probably just talk to you about this tomorrow." Weston looked as anxious to get out of here as I felt to explain myself.

"You came all the way here for a reason," I muttered. "Come on into the kitchen, and we'll chat."

Zeke nodded down the hallway. "I'll hop in the shower while you guys talk."

Weston's gaze remained on Zeke as he disappeared into the bathroom. Then he turned back to me. "So . . . you and Zeke?"

"It's not what it looks like," I explained. "Someone was following us tonight, and Zeke didn't feel right leaving me here by myself."

Weston slowly nodded, maybe even skeptically. "I see."

But I didn't think he saw anything at all—not the way I wanted him to, at least.

But I didn't need to explain my love life—or lack thereof—to Weston.

Instead, I nodded toward a chair at the kitchen table. "What brings you by?"

After he lowered himself at the table, I sat across from him. "Honestly? I just wanted to check on you."

I felt my heart softening. "That's really sweet of you. Thanks. Since you're here, how about if I make you some tea and fill you in on today's events?"

"I only have a couple minutes, but sure."

I wondered if that really was why Weston had stopped by. He'd started to tell me something earlier when Zeke first arrived. I wondered what he had on his mind.

But what I knew for certain was that now wasn't the time to ask.

A GOOGLE SEARCH the next morning led me to an article about two other moving scheme thefts in a two-hour vicinity of Savannah, and the write-ups even listed names of the victims. Another quick Google search led me to these people's current addresses.

I knew I wanted to talk to them. Thankfully, Zeke had been with me as I did my research and had offered to drive. He didn't seem to mind being my chauffeur—and bodyguard.

Still, it felt weird to be working with him like this and seeing him so often. In the past, Phil had always been with us, and Zeke and I being alone together now somehow felt off.

Yet, on the other hand, working with Zeke also sent a zing of excitement through me.

But it shouldn't.

I shook my head.

My emotions really confused me right now.

"You think this family you're meeting will have some information for you?" Zeke asked as he stared at the road ahead.

I shrugged. "I hope so. I won't know until I talk to them, I guess."

"You really are going after this, aren't you?"

I shrugged again. "The chancellor practically pushed this case on me. When I solved the last crime affiliated with the school, it was a great thing for the conservatory's publicity. I think Dr. Hannon is hoping this will do the same. Plus, the Abernathys are huge donors to the school. I'm sure Hannon wants to stay in their good graces."

"You're doing this on top of your other workload?"

"Thankfully, my other workload right now really only involves the Christmas fundraiser we're doing. In another week, the kids will be gone for Winter Break, and I'll have almost a month off. So, I suppose this is a rather slow season for me."

Zeke grunted.

"Although . . . Dr. Hannon *is* hoping that people will be making some last-minute donations to the nonprofit so they can get their end-of-the-year tax write-offs. I've been working with the head of alumni relations so we can send letters reminding people of that fact. We tweaked the wording so it won't sound so much like a sales pitch—I hope."

"It sounds like you're enjoying this new job."

"I am, much more so than I thought I would."

"What about Scarlett? What is she up to?"

At the sound of my daughter's name, I frowned. "She's dating someone. She sounds happy."

"That's good news, yes?"

"It's so hard to let them grow up, to let them fly on their own."

"But when you raise them right, you can rest a little easier."

His words brought me a strange comfort. "Yeah, I guess you're right. I also know that parenting an adult child is more challenging than I thought it would be."

"I can only imagine."

Zeke didn't have any kids. He'd been married for about ten years before his wife left him. I remembered how devastated he'd been and how he'd tried to win his wife back. But she'd met someone else and moved on. I suspected his failed marriage was the real reason he'd broken up with Carlena.

I remembered thinking how fortunate I was that Phil and I had such a wonderful marriage.

But what if we hadn't?

Moisture flooded my gaze, but I pulled it back before Zeke saw anything.

"What are you doing for Christmas?" I decided to change the subject.

He shrugged. "I haven't decided yet. The past several years I've spent the holidays with Carlena's family. Clearly, that's not going to happen this year."

"I understand. It's funny because there was a time in my life when I had so many places to be for Christmas that I thought I'd lose my mind. This year, it seems like there's nothing certain. I'm not sure how I feel about that."

Before we could talk about it anymore, we pulled up to a three-story house located in an upscale suburban area near Savannah.

I'd already called the Whitmores to see if I could meet with them. They'd said it was okay.

Now I hoped we would be able to gather some information on what was happening.

———

The Whitmores seemed to be a nice family. Alicia and John were probably in their early fifties with two teenagers still living at home. John was apparently an investment banker who made a pretty penny with his job.

They'd moved to this new house from another slightly smaller house only thirty minutes away.

They called this new place their dream home, one that they hadn't been able to walk away from when they saw it go on the market. I could see why. The place was located on ten acres and had a modern *Gone with the Wind* appearance.

However, the family hadn't expected the move to turn into such a nightmare.

Zeke and I were seated at a small table in the kitchen, and Alicia served us scones and hot tea. The whole house smelled like Christmas—evergreen and peppermint.

I found the scents comforting—kind of like I had at the coffeehouse.

I raised my teacup as I turned to Mrs. Whitmore. "If you don't mind me asking, where did you even hear about this moving company?"

"I did an online search, and they popped up." Mrs. Whitmore shrugged, her petite frame lean and fit, and her face smooth, absent from the normal signs of aging. "They had numerous good reviews, so I didn't think much about it. I called them, and they gave me a great quote."

"Did anyone from the company come over to look

at your house before giving you a quote?" Zeke asked.

"As a matter of fact, they did. The man who came seemed very professional and well-spoken. I didn't even think twice about trusting him, didn't even consider the idea that he might be a con artist."

"Most con artists are very good at what they do." Zeke pressed his lips together as if disturbed at the thought.

At the sound of the words "con artist," I felt my chest tighten. My dad was one of the world's most cunning con artists. He was now serving a life sentence in prison for all the crimes he'd committed.

The two of us hadn't spoken in years, and I had no intentions of speaking to him now.

This almost seemed like something he would orchestrate.

"So, someone came over, walked through the house, and gave you an estimate?" I repeated, trying to focus my thoughts again.

"That's right," Alicia said. "We set up the date and time. I paid half down. He showed up on time on the day of the move with all his workers, and they seemed to do a good job packing everything up. They said it would be two days until our items got to our new house, which I was assured was normal."

"Even though your new place was so close?" Zeke clarified.

She shrugged again. "I thought it was a little strange, but a couple more days didn't really matter. On the day our items were supposed to arrive, I waited here at the house, but they never showed up. I tried to call the movers, and they didn't answer their phone. That's when I started getting nervous."

"I bet." I tried to put myself into her shoes. She must have felt a sense of panic.

"Needless to say, I tried to call the company several more times. I had this guy's cell phone number. But I also had the number to the office. No one answered either number. Then I looked online for the address for the business. I went there, but the office space was empty. That's when I knew something was really wrong."

"So, you went to the police?" I nibbled my vanilla scone as I waited for her answer.

She nodded, her expression almost withdrawn. "I did, and they seemed clueless at first. I guess we were the first people in the area to experience this type of crime, and I'm not sure the police knew exactly what to do with that information. To be truthful, local law enforcement hasn't been extremely helpful. I know a house full of items probably isn't their first priority, but it's important to me."

I glanced around her house, which was currently furnished with upscale, designer furniture. "It looks like you had a happy ending."

"I did." Mrs. Whitmore frowned. "But only after I had to pay ten thousand dollars in ransom."

CHAPTER
FOURTEEN

MY EYES WIDENED at the number. "Ten thousand dollars? That's not cheap."

"These guys knew that," Alicia said. "They knew I'd pay whatever it took to get my items back. I know I can replace couches and chairs and tables. But it's more than that. These things were important to me."

"How did you make the payment?" Zeke tapped the side of his teacup.

"By wire transfer. I wasn't sure if that money would disappear, and I'd just be scammed again. But to my surprise, about five minutes after the money went through, I received an address."

"Did you go there?" I asked.

Mrs. Whitmore nodded quickly. "I did, even though I wasn't sure what I was going to find. Part of me feared I'd open the door only to discover another trap of some sort. But I was pleasantly surprised to find all my items were inside."

"Did you talk to anyone working at the facility?" Zeke asked.

"I talked to a couple of people there. But, truthfully, I was just happy to have all my possessions back. At that point, I knew there wasn't a good chance of me tracking these guys down. They were good at what they did."

"Can I have the name of that storage facility?" I asked.

"Of course."

As Mrs. Whitmore rattled it off, I typed it into my phone.

Zeke's gaze still looked intense, like he was determined to get to the bottom of this. "Were the police involved in any part of that?"

"We told them what was going on, but that was pretty much the extent of their involvement. I don't wish for anyone else to go through what I did. That's why I agreed to do that interview with the newspaper—so I could try to warn people. But, like I said, these guys are good. They just set up new company names, phone numbers, and storefronts, and they recreate themselves. That's how they keep doing this without being caught."

"Could you describe to me what this guy looked like who came to your house?" Zeke continued.

"He was thirty-something and professional with a bit of a Northeastern accent, maybe like someone from Boston might have. He dressed well and seemed to be efficient."

Boston accent? This was definitely the same guy.

My pulse quickened. "Do you by chance have any images of the man? Maybe from a doorbell camera or something?"

She frowned and shook her head. "I wish I did. But, no, I don't have anything, unfortunately."

I nodded and thanked her. What she'd shared with us wasn't much to go on. But a clearer picture was forming in my head. And I was thankful for that at least.

———

"What now, boss?" Zeke asked as we climbed back into his SUV.

I kind of liked being called boss.

"Now we go to the storage facility, of course." I did a double take at Zeke as I realized I was assuming an awful lot right now. Zeke clearly had other things he needed to do. "Unless you're busy and can't drive all the way out there. I know Mrs.

Whitmore said it was about forty-five minutes away."

The corner of his lip curled up in a smile. "I'm game. I feel like I'm just as invested in this now as you are. It's really an intriguing scam these guys have going on."

"I'd say." I crossed my arms and stared out the window. "What still perplexes me is the fact that these guys actually killed someone. As it stood before, what they were doing was a simple theft. But, now, it's a violent crime. What caused the change?"

Zeke stared out the window a moment in thought. "The only thing that makes sense is that the man who died tried to turn the tables on these guys. Maybe he threatened to either turn the other guys in or take the violin when he realized it was valuable. There's really no telling at this point."

"If I understand correctly, these guys have already hit about five different families within a three-hour vicinity of Savannah."

"You're right. The pattern I'm seeing indicates they'll keep doing this for as long as they can."

That was my thought as well. "What Mrs. Whitmore said was right. Although this is serious, the police still have other crimes to attend to, crimes that are more life-threatening."

Zeke stole a glance at me. "Any word if the FBI is going to get involved?"

"Not that anyone has told me. But having a Stradivari violin stolen will take this to another level. It won't surprise me if they get involved."

"I agree."

He started his SUV, and we rode down the road in silence. As we did, my thoughts continued to turn over everything I'd learned.

Tracking down these guys was going to be hard. But I was determined to do what I could.

I had most of the day to work on this. At six this evening, we had another rehearsal for The Christmas Thing. I'd do what I could until then.

For the rest of the ride, Zeke and I chatted about our mutual friends in Atlanta and shared bittersweet memories of times we'd spent together with Phil and Carlena. It almost seemed like another lifetime ago.

Yet life went on, and here we were now.

Finally, we pulled up at Do-It-Right Storage. Zeke parked, and we strode inside the office together.

I hoped an answer might be found here.

But, unfortunately, another part of me seriously doubted it.

"YEAH, I REMEMBER THAT INCIDENT," a gruff man standing behind the counter told us. "That was just crazy to think they stole an entire house full of stuff and held it hostage."

The thin, lanky man was probably around my age, though he seemed much older—in my mind, at least. His light-brown hair was thinning, premature wrinkles showed he'd lived hard, and yellowed teeth made me think he was a smoker.

A name tag read, "Roger."

I leaned toward the counter. "Do you remember anything about the guys who stored the items here? About when they came in to reserve the storage unit?"

Roger shrugged. "Honestly, we've had so many people coming in and out of here. I try to pay attention because I don't want anything illegal happening. But these guys seemed legit. They didn't cause any trouble or make a ruckus. I figured they were just moving items into a storage facility for one of their clients."

"They give you a name?" I asked.

"They did. The police took it." Roger shrugged. "Don't matter, though. It was an alias."

"Too bad." I fought disappointment at what appeared to be a dead end. "What about video surveillance? Did you happen to get any of these guys?"

"Yeah, I gave that to the police also."

"Do you still have a copy?" Intimidating Zeke appeared again, and he glowered over the man behind the desk, apparently impatient with the man's lackadaisical attitude.

"Maybe." Roger shrugged again, not seeming to care.

I stepped closer, knowing I needed to get this guy on our side. "Can you think of anything that might help us? It's really important."

The man shook his head. "Don't think so."

"We're wasting our time here, Camryn." Zeke spoke up looking even more impatient.

"Camryn?" Roger paused and squinted at me. "Wait . . . I know you."

"Me?" I couldn't remember ever meeting this guy before.

"Yeah . . . you're Camryn Paine, the singer, aren't you?"

I swallowed hard, knowing I was about to use my former celebrity status to advance this case. Was that wrong? I wasn't sure.

But I wasn't going to let this opportunity pass.

"I am."

Suddenly, Roger's entire demeanor changed. "I went to five of your concerts between high school and college."

"Wow." I placed my hand over my heart. "I'm flattered."

He reached beneath the counter and pulled out an old photo of me wearing skintight pants and an over-sized pink sweatshirt. "I even keep this with me."

I swallowed hard as I stared at the old photo. The fact that he'd kept it with him all these years . . . it gave me a new perspective on the man. Made me wonder if he was a little off-balance.

"I . . . I don't even know what to say," I finally stuttered.

"I'll tell you whatever you want." He pushed the picture toward me. "If you'll sign this."

"Of course, I will." I exchanged a look with Zeke, who appeared to be holding back a smile.

Once Roger had the photo in hand and a dopey grin on his face, he turned back to us. He suddenly seemed *very* helpful and eager. "So, what do you need to know?"

"The video?" I reminded him.

"Of course." He nodded, long and slow. "I saved a couple of copies, just in case."

"Can we have one?" I sent him a hopeful glance.

"I don't see why not. I don't want my facility being associated with things like this happening. So, if you talk to the media or do anything like that, just leave me out of this. Please. Even you, Camryn Paine." He winked at me.

"I will." I grinned, even though I wasn't necessarily enjoying his attention. "I promise."

He gave me one last look before heading into an office. A moment later, he came out with a jump drive. "Maybe this is old-school, but it's all I've got. The video is on here."

"Thank you."

"No—thank *you.*" He winked again as if all his college fantasies were coming true.

Armed with that information, Zeke and I headed out to his SUV. As soon as we climbed inside, he grabbed a laptop from the backseat and turned it on.

"I want one of those photos like Roger has of you

from back in the day. Or, better yet, a poster. If I find one, will you autograph it for me too?"

I punched Zeke in the shoulder. "Very funny."

He grinned as he plugged in the jump drive, and we watched for several minutes until the images of these guys appeared.

There were three men. In one shot, I could nearly make out one of their faces. "Can you take a screenshot of that one?"

"Exactly what I was thinking too," Zeke said.

I stared at the image of a Caucasian man with a dark beard and shaded eyes.

It wasn't much, but at least it was something.

Maybe if I spread this image around, I would get some answers. "Ready to go?"

Zeke nodded. Just as he started his SUV, a new sound cut through the air.

I swallowed a scream when I realized it was a gunshot.

CHAPTER
SIXTEEN

"GET DOWN!" Zeke threw himself over me.

Glass shattered like a hailstorm around us.

I held my breath, waiting to see what would happen next.

Would this person keep shooting? Would they approach the SUV to ensure that they hit their mark?

Blood roared in my ears as I waited.

Then I heard tires squeal.

Several minutes later—or maybe it was only seconds—Zeke lifted himself from overtop me. He kept a hand on my back to keep me down as he glanced around.

"Are they gone?" My voice shook as I asked the question. My life had flashed before my eyes, and I still halfway expected a bullet to come from nowhere and pierce me.

"That's how it looks."

As I rose, shards of glass fell from my hair and clothing. My heart pounded out of control. My lungs still felt tight.

"Should we go after them?" My voice cracked as I asked the question.

Zeke shook his head. "It's too late. Plus, I can't drive with my windshield like this. It isn't safe."

I stared at his once-immaculate SUV and shook my head. "I'm so sorry. I feel like this is my fault."

He turned toward me, his eyes softening. "This isn't your fault, Camryn."

Something about the concern in his voice made my breath catch.

But this was no time to wonder if romance could possibly be in my future—especially not with Zeke. He was my husband's friend.

Just because he was here and protective and attentive . . . that didn't mean anything.

Only that he was being a good friend to Phil.

I cleared my throat, chastising myself for the thought. "Do you think this has to do with Phil?"

"That's my best guess."

I shook my head before letting out a sigh. "Just what did he get himself wrapped up in?"

"I'd like to know that also."

I locked my jaw in place.

I'd been trying to be quiet and not ask too many questions.

But no more.

Now I wanted answers.

Especially now that it was apparent my life was on the line.

———

Thirty minutes later, Garrison had taken our statements.

A witness from two blocks down had said they saw a dark SUV driving away at the time of the gunshots. They hadn't gotten a license plate, however.

A tow truck had come, and Zeke and I were now riding to a repair shop. Then we'd pick up a rental car from there.

I glanced at my watch. I still had three hours until I needed to be at the rehearsal. This definitely wasn't the way I'd planned on spending my afternoon.

"I'm glad you're okay," Zeke said when we were finally in the rental car.

I pushed a hair behind my ear, and another piece of glass fell out. It seemed like every time I moved, I found another shard. "Thanks. I just can't believe this is happening."

"I know."

I turned toward him, my voice somber as I said, "We need to talk, Zeke. To really talk. There's something I should probably tell you about."

I hadn't mentioned Phil's possible affair. But what if it was connected? I had to tell Zeke, even if it meant opening up a can of worms I would rather pretend didn't exist. Even if it meant feeling humiliated and betrayed and foolish.

His jaw tightened. "Why don't we stop and grab a bite to eat? I can still have you back at Grand Isle in time for your rehearsal tonight."

I nodded, dreading how this conversation would go. But I had no other choice right now.

A few minutes later, we pulled into a little diner on the side of the road. It was nothing fancy—a single story building, painted white, with blue shutters and a small, cheerful snowflake flag that flapped in the wind in the otherwise barren flowerbeds.

Places like this usually had good comfort food, but I wasn't sure how much I was going to be able to eat. My stomach was churning too hard.

SEVENTEEN

AFTER THE WAITRESS had delivered our shrimp and grits, I turned to Zeke. "I didn't make this connection at first. But now I'm thinking maybe I should have. If I'd paid more attention . . ."

He took a long sip of his sweet tea and placed it back on the table before locking his gaze with mine. "What connection?"

I swallowed hard. I hadn't dared to speak these words aloud before. But I couldn't hide what I'd discovered anymore.

"I pulled out a box of Christmas decorations last week," I started. "At the bottom of the box, I found an old jump drive. I guess it just fell in there when I was packing away the Christmas stuff one year. I didn't think much of it. Then, out of curiosity, I plugged it into my computer."

"What was on it?"

"Some old emails Phil had sent. It was . . ." My voice caught, and I rubbed my throat. "The emails were all between Phil and a woman named Andrea Philips."

Zeke's intense gaze nearly shot laser beams into me. "What did the messages say?"

I shrugged, feeling an invisible weight pressing into my body. "They were all vague, to be honest. He talked about seeing her again." A lump formed in my throat.

"Camryn . . ."

My gaze locked with his. "Was Phil cheating on me, Zeke?"

I didn't look away. I didn't want to give him a chance to lie. If anyone knew the answer to that question, it was Zeke.

"No." His word sounded confident, like he wasn't trying to bluff. "Phil wasn't cheating on you."

"How do you know?" I studied his face, unable to look away. I needed to see the truth.

I needed to hear it in his voice.

Zeke didn't break his gaze. "Because I knew Phil. He would never do something like that."

I wanted to believe that also. But could I?

I leaned back and crossed my arms. "Then I have no idea what those emails could mean."

"Can I see them? Maybe they're connected with what's going on now."

I nodded, already dreading having to share them. "When we get back to my apartment tonight, yes."

Zeke leaned forward and lowered his voice. "Does anyone know you found the emails?"

"I actually . . . I tried to call Andrea." I shrugged, feeling even more foolish to admit it. "I found an address for her, and I was curious, I guess. But her landlady answered and told me that Andrea had . . . she died."

"When?"

I rubbed my throat, trying to get rid of the ache there. "A week before Phil did."

Zeke visibly stiffened. "Why didn't you tell me earlier? What if their deaths are connected? This could be the link I've been looking for."

I pressed my lips together, hating how tense my body felt. Hating all the noises around me—the other diners chatting. Their silverware hitting their plates. The Christmas music dancing through small speakers in the corner. Bacon sizzling from the kitchen.

Yet, at the same time, the noises brought me comfort. They gave me a sense of privacy. They muted what we were talking about.

I glanced back at Zeke. "I felt humiliated. I probably would have told you sooner, but I was still processing."

"You have no reason to feel humiliated. Even if Phil had cheated, that would be on him. He would have been crazy to leave you for someone else."

My cheeks heated. That almost sounded like a compliment.

I pushed those thoughts aside. "Do you think . . . when I made that call and asked about Andrea . . . it set something in motion?"

Zeke stared into the distance before shrugging. "That's the only thing that makes sense to me."

So, who was Andrea Philips? What was Phil's relationship with her?

And why would someone kill Phil as a result?

I'd looked into the woman. She didn't work for Bromtech, and she wasn't from Charleston. But, certainly, there could be other connections . . .

I played with the rest of my food, knowing the little bit of appetite I had left was gone after this conversation.

I glanced at my watch. "We should probably get going."

The sooner Zeke saw the emails, the sooner I might have some answers. But, first, I needed to get back to the school.

————

"You look like you've seen a ghost," Weston said as we sat in the front row during The Christmas Thing rehearsal.

That was the thing about Weston. He was always observant. Even when I tried to hide how I was really feeling, he seemed to notice.

"It's been one of those days." I frowned and folded my arms across my chest as I remembered being shot at. As I replayed my conversation with Zeke.

"If you ever need to talk, I'm here." Sincerity etched his words, and I knew he meant them.

Plus, Weston was a good listener.

But did I really want to pull him into this mess with Phil? It probably wasn't a good idea.

Besides, this wasn't the time. Right now, we had twenty different acts getting ready to rehearse. We had less than a week until the big performance, and I needed to give this all my energy.

I turned back to the stage as the next set of performers took their places.

The kids at the school were so talented. That was evident in the acts that they'd put together. There were both classic and original numbers. Solos. Duets. Ensembles.

Each one was top-notch.

I couldn't wait to splice in some of the interviews we'd done yesterday. When I got into the office tomorrow morning, that was what I would work on.

As the rehearsal came to an end, all the performers gathered onstage to take their bows.

"This has been great, but we're missing something." Beck Tarsus stepped from the group. He was one of the star musicians here at the school, someone I truly saw as having a long career in music.

"What's that?" Weston asked.

"You two should do a duet," Beck said. "That would really get people coming."

I shook my head at the mere thought. "That's not a good idea."

"People would go crazy if you two had a reunion and sang one of your songs."

"I'm not so sure about that," I quickly countered, fighting a strange sense of panic.

"It's not a bad idea." Weston shrugged and readjusted his cowboy hat.

My eyes widened as I looked at him. That wasn't what I had expected him to say.

But the thought of working with Weston again . . . of stirring up all those old memories . . . it seemed like a terrible idea.

"I don't know." I shook my head.

Then all the kids onstage started chanting, "Do it."

Finally, I laughed. "I'll think about it. How about that?"

"It's a good start." Weston flashed a smile at me.

I wanted to shake my head again. A duet wasn't something I'd expected to be asked to do, especially not from this generation. I figured most of my fans were now old enough to be carting their kids to sporting events or getting them ready for college.

I thought I'd put this old part of my life behind me.

So why did my past want to become part of my future again?

I MOSTLY AVOIDED Weston as we cleaned up after the rehearsal. I didn't want him to talk anymore about doing the duet. I needed time to sort things out first.

When Skittles came into the room, that was the perfect excuse to avoid him.

"Any updates on the Abernathys? I was just talking to Tara earlier, and she was wondering."

I paused and sat on the edge of the stage, so I wasn't looming over Skittles. "We've made some headway, but not as much as I hoped. However, I do have a better image of one of our suspects. I just need to figure out how I can identify him."

"I can post it on social media."

I glanced at Skittles and let out a skeptical grunt. "I'm not sure that's a good idea."

"I think it's a *great* idea. I can ask my friends to share and then their friends can share and, before you know it, we'll probably have tips rolling in."

"You really think?" I considered myself fairly social media savvy. But this topic didn't seem like something tons of people would want to share.

"That seems like a good possibility. Social media is the new Crimeline and *America's Most Wanted*. Trust me—I just read a social media post about it."

Maybe she had a point. *Maybe.* But there were other things to consider.

"Skittles, I appreciate your offer. But I don't want to put you in the middle of this, especially not now that someone is dead."

"I understand. But, honestly, I think it would be okay. It's at least worth a shot."

I stared at her hopeful expression. "I'll tell you what—let me craft a press release first—with Mrs. Abernathy's permission, of course. If that doesn't work, we'll look into your idea."

Skittles grinned. "That sounds perfect."

I added one more thing to my to-do list.

After everyone cleared out, only Weston and I were left in the auditorium.

He paused in front of me as we lingered near the stage, picking up some props that had been left out. He took the piece of red garland and wrapped it around my neck like a boa.

He winked. "It's a good look."

I laughed and struck a pose. "I'm sure."

His gaze lingered on me a moment before he stepped back and rubbed his neck.

"What do you think about the kids' idea?" He stuffed his hands into the front pockets of his jeans, thumbs poking out in a picture-worthy stance.

I frowned as I remembered their chants of "Do it, do it." "Honestly? I think it's terrible."

Weston's gaze probed into mine, a trace of surprise lingering in the depths of his deep brown eyes. "Why is that?"

My throat tightened.

I didn't really want to go into all my explanations with him. But since he'd directly asked me . . . "That part of my life is done. Why dredge up memories?"

Something seemed to close in his gaze, and he stepped back—almost as if he'd sealed off some secret emotions, locking them away for safekeeping.

"I understand." Resignation stained his voice.

Was he asking for deeper reasons? When I said that part of my life was done, did he think I was talking about him? Even more so . . . was I?

My throat burned. I didn't know the answer to those questions.

Weston started to take another step back when he stopped and stared at me again. "Those old times weren't all bad, were they?"

I felt my heart softening when I heard the earnestness in his voice. "No, they weren't. Not at all. In fact, some of my fondest memories go back to . . . us."

Hope seemed to ignite in his eyes again. "Mine too."

We stared at each other a moment, something passing between us.

Until someone cleared their throat in the distance.

I jerked my head toward the sound, still remembering those earlier gunshots. My body tensed as I went into fight-or-flight mode.

But instead of seeing danger, I spotted Zeke standing at the back of Hannon Auditorium.

"I hope I'm not interrupting." He strode down the aisle toward me. "But, after everything that happened today, I thought it was a good idea if I drove you home."

"Everything that happened today?" Weston turned back to me, a wrinkle between his eyes.

"Someone shot at us," I explained.

His eyes widened. "What?"

Zeke strode down the aisle and met us. "Everything turned out okay. But the police still haven't caught the person behind it."

"This is all because of some supposed movers stealing people's possessions?" Weston's words came out fast and almost heated.

He was worried, wasn't he?

His concern was sweet.

"Not really. I don't think so, at least." I exchanged a look with Zeke.

Realization seemed to spread over Weston's features, and he slowly nodded. "Phil?"

I nodded.

Weston studied me, his gaze practically propelling me toward him.

I had the feeling he wanted to pull me into a hug.

But he didn't.

Probably because Zeke was here.

Instead, he kept his hands in his front pockets and nodded. "I see."

"I know there's a lot to talk about, but . . ." Zeke nodded toward the door. "We should probably go."

I cast one more glance at Weston. "We'll catch up later, okay?"

His jaw flexed. "Yes, we should definitely do that. I'll finish up here and see you in the morning."

I WOKE up the next morning with a brilliant idea.

I could hardly get dressed fast enough. As soon as I was ready, I hurried into the kitchen to share my brainstorm with Zeke.

He was already dressed and sitting at the kitchen table with a cup of coffee. Of course, I'd known that he was. I'd heard the pounding water of the shower. Heard the coffeepot gurgling. Had heard Zeke grabbing a mug from the cabinet.

As usual, he was a sight to behold in a very understated kind of way—jeans, a long-sleeved black shirt, clean-shaven face, and perfect hair.

How was it fair that men simply looked more distinguished as they got older while women were, in general, considered less attractive?

"Good morning." Zeke's gaze drifted up and down with approval.

"I have an idea," I announced as I grabbed some coffee and sat across from him.

Curiosity danced in his eyes. "I can't wait to hear."

"As you probably know, I still have the house back in Atlanta. I don't know exactly what I want to do with it yet, but I'm not ready to sell. But I could pretend that I am and—"

"That's a terrible idea." Zeke's gaze sliced into mine.

I frowned. "I haven't finished yet."

His stoic, no-nonsense expression remained. "But I know what you're going to say. You're going to say you could hire some movers to move your things here to Savannah."

"Exactly. I think it's a *great* idea." Why wouldn't he think so?

Zeke let his head fall to the side as if he hated breaking this news to me. "You don't want to get yourself mixed up in the middle of these guys."

"I think this is the perfect way to figure out who they are."

He shook his head, his expression unyielding. "I don't want you to get hurt."

"Who says I'm going to get hurt? These guys probably don't even know who I am. And I have the perfect cover story if they look into me. I'm working here in Savannah, but my stuff is in Atlanta."

He glanced at my apartment. "But your place is already furnished."

"I can move a few things from Atlanta into a storage facility. Not only that, but I can put tracking devices on some of my possessions. That way we'll know exactly what these guys are doing with them."

Zeke narrowed his eyes, clearly still skeptical. "You don't think these guys are getting wise to that?"

"They've already struck several times, and they have a good thing going. It's like you said, they're going to want to keep at it."

He frowned. "Do you plan on telling the police about your plan?"

"I haven't decided. I mean, these guys have struck in different states—they're smart like that. So, there's a good chance all the police departments working these crimes haven't communicated with each other."

"Very true."

"I suppose I could tell Garrison, however. You think I should do this?"

He stared at me another moment before shrugging again. "Not really, but I'm not sure I could stop you even if I wanted to."

He was right. He couldn't.

————

Back at work, I hung up the phone and frowned. My phone calls hadn't been working out the way I'd hoped.

I'd called six different moving companies, but none of the people I spoke to had matched the voice I heard on the doorbell video.

I sighed and grabbed a package of baby carrots I'd brought with me. I picked one up and dipped it into the small container of mustard.

I still had four other companies to call, but I was beginning to feel discouraged.

Maybe these people were waiting longer between their jobs so they wouldn't be caught. That's what a smart criminal might do. But I wasn't convinced they were that smart.

Then again, I could do all this, and it could be for nothing. Besides, didn't I have enough going on without driving back to Atlanta to stage this whole operation? The answer to that was a resounding yes.

Someone knocked at the door, and I looked up to see Joseph standing there. I plastered on a smile as I braced myself for whatever he had to say. Usually, my talks with him ended with me feeling apprehensive.

"How are you, Joseph?"

"I'm doing well." He rubbed his hands together, looking insincerely enthusiastic. "I saw the news story this morning on the moving company scam. Good job with that. Hopefully you'll get some hits."

I'd sent out the press release and talked to a reporter late last night. I'd seen a clip of the story as I perused the news this morning. "I'm hopeful also."

He shifted. "I was wondering if you had any updates on the Abernathys?"

The *real* reason he was here. "I'm working on things, but I don't have any answers yet."

I didn't bother to tell him that my whole life felt as if it had been turned upside down.

I decided not to tell him about my sting operation that I was trying to set up. The less people who knew about that, the better.

"Did you send out the follow-up letters for the fundraiser yet?"

I glanced at that notation on my to-do list. "I have a meeting in an hour about that. It will get done. I promise."

He nodded, seeming as if he trusted me. He should. I hadn't let him down yet.

"How is The Christmas Thing going?"

I looked at my computer screen where I'd been working on cleaning up the video interviews Weston and I had done. I needed to work on them more today, but we had some great footage.

"We had another rehearsal last night," I told him. "I thought it went really well."

"That's good news, at least."

I thought our conversation might be finished, but Joseph made no effort to move.

Instead, his gaze fastened on mine. "I just wanted to let you know that I think you're doing a really good job here at the school, Camryn."

I blinked in surprise. I hadn't expected the compliment. "Thank you. I'm honored that you asked me to come work for you."

"Your reputation preceded you. Everyone I talked to on your reference sheet highly recommended you. You have a way of putting a positive spin on situations. That's truly admirable."

That was a good thing . . . right? Part of me didn't want to consider myself a spin doctor, but I suppose that *was* what I did.

Finally, after staring at me another moment, Joseph straightened. "I'll let you get back to work. It sounds like you have a lot to do."

After he left the room, I released the breath that I hadn't even realized I had been holding.

I glanced at my desk again.

I needed to get back to my to-do list . . . because right now I felt like I wasn't getting anything accomplished.

AFTER I FINISHED WORKING on the video, I stood and stretched my legs.

The rehearsal last night filled my head, and I remembered the students chanting that Weston and I should sing together again.

Onstage.

In public.

I dropped back into my seat.

I still felt gun-shy at the thought.

Out of curiosity, I pulled up an old video on my computer of a concert Weston and I had done together. I fast-forwarded until I reached "Me and You," a song that Weston and I had sung as a duet, and I braced myself.

We stepped onto the stage, walked toward each other, our gazes locked in the ultimate display of dramatics. As we raised our microphones and prepared to sing, the crowd went crazy.

The camera panned to the audience, and there were tears in some people's eyes as they reached their hands in the air and watched our every move.

It was show business at its best.

I could hardly breathe as I watched myself begin singing the first line.

It was a night unlike any other.

I was lost, alone, yet somehow smothered.

Then you appeared

Like an answer to prayer.

As Weston began his verse, he stepped closer to me.

By the time we reached the chorus, we were face-to-face.

He reached for my hand.

The crowd went wild.

The look in both of our eyes was nothing short of adoration for each other. That hadn't been faked. Our affection was all real, and everyone watching knew it.

That concert was three months before our breakup, a breakup that had shattered my heart into a million pieces.

I'd seen my future being with Weston, and when I

realized that wasn't going to happen, I'd barely been able to pull myself back together.

An ache gripped my heart at the memory of those broken dreams—broken dreams that had led to a broken Camryn.

"You're thinking about doing that song together, aren't you?"

As a voice filled the room, I quickly closed my computer. My heart pounded out of control.

Skittles stood in my doorway, a handful of yellow candy in her palm. She broadcast her moods by what color she ate. Yellow usually meant happy.

Had I been so absorbed in that video that I hadn't heard her coming?

I was losing my touch.

Either way, I released the breath I held.

I raised my chin, trying to make it clear that I didn't appreciate her interruption. "I didn't say I was considering it. I was just . . ."

What *was* I doing? I couldn't even think of a good excuse.

"It's okay if you don't want to admit it." Skittles grinned as she stared at me. "I think a duet would be *great*. Fantastic. Memorable. It would knock this whole event out of the ballpark—"

I raised my hand, silently begging for her to stop.

"I get it. But things are a lot more complicated than that."

"Because you used to love Weston."

I frowned at her words, but I couldn't deny them. "I was very much in love with him back then. But that was more than twenty years ago."

"Maybe fate has brought you back together again."

I resisted a cynical snicker. "I don't believe in fate."

"Maybe you should." Skittles stared at me as if trying to read my thoughts.

Instead, I gave her a pointed look. "Is that what you came to talk to me about?"

She seemed to snap out of her daze. "No, of course not. I came to tell you that I just talked to Mrs. Abernathy."

"And?"

"She told me the FBI is getting involved in this case. She just got the call from them."

Why did disappointment press on me at that news? "Well, that's probably good. They'll be able to find answers much faster than I can."

"Yet, at the same time, you don't want them to win." She continued to stare at me as if she could read my mind.

"This has nothing to do with me. Besides, solving

this case isn't a competition."

"Maybe it should be. *That* could make for some good reality TV. The professionals versus the amateurs." She used her best announcer voice as she dramatically stared into space.

"A show like that would be interesting, but I'm afraid I wouldn't stand a chance."

"If you have that Zeke guy helping you, you might. Who would've thought that Camryn Paine would have *two* men chasing after her?" She wagged her eyebrows as if my love life was her biggest source of entertainment right now.

I gave her a look that hopefully made it clear I was losing my patience. As much as I liked Skittles, she wasn't my friend. She worked for me—and she was my daughter's age.

"No one is chasing after me," I finally said. "You're reading entirely too much into this situation. Let's get back to the subject at hand. You said the FBI is getting involved?"

Her expression turned serious—almost mockingly so. "Yeah, Mrs. Abernathy told me that she wants you to call her sometime."

"Why didn't she just call me herself?"

"I couldn't tell you. Maybe you should call her and find out."

It looked like I was going to have to do that.

———

As soon as Skittles left, I picked up the phone to call Mrs. Abernathy. She answered on the second ring and must have had my number programmed because she knew who I was before I said a word.

"Hello, Mrs. Paine."

"Hi, Mrs. Abernathy. I was told you had an update for me."

"I do. I just got a call from Detective Garrison, and he informed me that the Art Crime Team with the FBI will be getting involved with this case. I thought you'd like to know."

"That's good news, right? They have many more resources than I do."

"I suppose they do. But I'd still like for you to work this case."

I blinked with surprise at her words. "I'm sure the FBI will get much farther than I can."

"But I believe in *you*. I have a gut feeling you're going to figure this out. Speaking of which, are there any updates I should know about?"

I told her everything I'd learned and, just for fun, gave her the inside scoop on what I was planning.

"Clever." Admiration stretched through her voice. "I like the way you think. Just don't put yourself in any danger, Camryn." Her voice took on a motherly tone.

"I don't plan on doing that. I have my eyes wide open. Believe me."

"Keep me updated. As you can imagine, my family and I are anxious to get our items back."

I paused before asking, "No ransom calls yet?"

"The man with the FBI said there very well may not be a ransom call in this situation. The previous victims didn't have a valuable violin in their possession. These guys will make more off that instrument than they will the ransom demand. That doesn't make me very happy."

I frowned, even though that theory made a lot of sense. "Does insurance even cover this?"

"From what I have been told, no." Her words sounded clipped.

I frowned. "I'll keep you updated."

"I look forward to hearing from you. By the way, come to dinner at my house tonight. Bring someone with you." Her words were spoken almost as a command more than a request.

"Tonight?" I scrambled to think of a response. It was one of those "I loved being invited but hated actually going" type of moments—especially since I had so many other things on my mind right now.

"No excuses. Be there at seven. Toodle-oo!"

I supposed that was that.

I was going to dinner at the Abernathys' tonight. Maybe it would be good for me to keep my mind occupied.

As soon as I ended the call with Mrs. Abernathy, I pulled up the names of the other moving companies I'd listed. I might as well give them a call right now also.

A woman answered at the first company.

I scratched their name off my list. No one had mentioned a woman being involved with this.

But the second company I called, a man answered.

A man with a slight Boston accent.

Did I finally have my *Bingo!* moment? I could only hope.

CHAPTER
TWENTY-ONE

"I'M SORRY, but I don't have any availability until tomorrow at the earliest but most likely the day after."

I nibbled on my bottom lip. "I'm afraid I'm in a hurry and I'm talking to other companies."

"If they have earlier availability, then go with them. I'm sorry. But we're just really backed up right now."

"I understand." I needed to book whatever I could before I missed this opportunity. "I'll take your next availability then."

"Great. Text me with your address, and I'll text you back to let you know when I can come. Right now, we'll plan on six o'clock tomorrow evening. But, just to let you know, that could change."

Six o'clock tomorrow evening? Did I have something going on then?

Whatever it was, I would try to reschedule.

"That sounds perfect. Thank you."

I ended the call and felt a strange sense of excitement rising in me.

Until I glanced at my window and saw someone peering inside.

———

As soon as the man saw me looking at him, he took off in a run.

I couldn't let him get away.

Before I could second-guess myself, I sprinted from my office and down the hall. But by the time I reached the outside, he was nowhere to be seen.

I stood there and frowned, trying to figure out where he might have gone and wondering if there was any chance I could catch him.

I didn't think so.

I hadn't seen his face. He'd been wearing a mask.

Had anyone else seen him? And what was he doing by my window? What had he hoped to accomplish?

I glanced around, but no one seemed to be paying attention.

Instead, I walked to my window to see if he'd left anything behind.

I knew it was a long shot, but I figured it was worth looking.

I paused there. There was a photo on the ground.

A photo of me.

———

By the time four o'clock rolled around, my body was telling me it was time to go home. There was something about sitting at a desk all day that just didn't agree with me. My body liked to move, to be active. Maybe that was why I'd enjoyed the toddler years so much. Chasing a little one around the house had just felt natural.

As a shadow filled my doorway, I looked over and saw Professor Amile standing there.

"Professor . . . how are you doing?"

It was almost as if he didn't hear my question. "I saw something I thought you might want to know about."

"What's that?"

"I like to scan ads in the different classical music magazines online. I saw that someone wanted to sell a Stradivari violin." He handed me a printout. "I thought you might want to see this."

My eyes widened when I read the classified ad. "Do you think that this is the violin I'm looking for?"

"It's hard to say. I'm not saying that you should go meet this person who's selling it. But I did think that you should know about it, just in case. It would be terrible if a violin like that got into the wrong hands—the hands of someone who didn't appreciate it."

"I agree. Thank you for sharing this with me."

He nodded. "No problem."

I glanced down at the ad again.

Could this be it?

There was only one way to find out.

I dialed the number to see if I might be able to check it out.

TWENTY-TWO

TO MY SURPRISE, the person selling the violin texted me right after I tried to call. He said he couldn't talk at the moment, so I responded that I was interested in the violin.

Now we had a meeting at Emmet Park in an hour.

My stomach squeezed at the thought.

I knew I couldn't go alone. It wouldn't be smart.

But Zeke was meeting with Bromarski today.

That's when I called Weston.

Thankfully, he didn't have any plans, and he always seemed up for an adventure.

That was how the two of us had ended up walking toward the park together right now.

It seemed like even when I wanted to avoid this man, our paths kept leading us back to each other.

As we walked, images of our time together in

Savannah as students filled my mind. We'd actually gone to this park one time. Weston had pulled out his guitar, and we'd sung songs together. A local promoter had walked by and heard us. He'd eventually asked us to play as an opening act at a local venue. After that, things had really taken off in our careers.

We'd both been so young and hopeful back then. We hadn't realized the toll fame would take on us. Hadn't realized how our lives would seem destined to go in different directions. Hadn't realized the heartache we would endure all in the name of living.

"What are you thinking about?" Weston's voice pulled me from my thoughts.

I shoved my hands into the pockets of my army-green jacket as I soaked in the sprawling oak trees draped with Spanish moss. "I'm thinking about when you and I first started in music. Sometimes those seem like the good old days. People think that the good days will happen once you arrive, once you reach a certain level of success. But I've always found that beginnings usually contain the most joy."

"Maybe you should write a song about it."

I let out a chuckle and shook my head. "I haven't written a song in . . . years."

"But you have a talent for it."

"Maybe. But sometimes writing songs requires

opening up old wounds." I wasn't sure that was something I was prepared to do. The wounds seemed to open up just fine on their own.

"Our pain is usually what makes music touch others."

Weston's words hung in the air. I couldn't deny them. But did I really want to capitalize on what I'd been through?

I didn't think so.

"My producer is trying to talk me into doing a Christmas tour," Weston said after a few minutes of silence.

I jerked my head toward him in surprise. "Isn't it a little bit late for that?"

"I'd be joining Mark Johnson in his current tour. I would kind of work myself into it."

"But Christmas is only three weeks away."

"This tour actually starts two weeks before Christmas and goes right up until Christmas Eve."

I slowed my steps in order to draw out this conversation. "So, what are you going to do?"

"I'm still thinking about it. But it's tempting. It's not like I'm going to see my kids anyway."

Compassion welled in me. "I'm sorry. I know that must be hard for you."

He shrugged, even though I could tell it was bothering him. "Yeah, well, that's life, right?"

I wanted to argue with the statement, but I couldn't. That just seemed to be the course life took sometimes. We could spend all our energy fighting it or we could just simply pave a different way.

I looked ahead and saw the spot we were meeting the seller.

I braced myself as I wondered what was going to play out here in a second.

———

Instead of going right to the bench where we were supposed to meet, Weston and I lingered near a tree, just out of sight. Anyone passing would just think we were two friends—or possibly lovers—enjoying some time together.

I looked over as I saw someone walking our way. His shadowed face made it hard to make out any of his features, but he did carry a violin case.

As he looked up and the light caught his gaze, something about his gaze indicated he was the person we were supposed to meet.

I gripped Weston's arm, silently signaling that we needed to be on guard.

"Aren't you Weston Turner?" someone yelled behind us.

I twirled around in time to see four twenty-something women gaping at Weston.

His eyes widened and he sucked in a breath, instantly going into deer-in-the-headlights mode.

They rushed toward him, stars in their eyes. "Oh my gosh! It's Weston Turner. Can we have your autograph?"

I glanced back over at the man with the violin.

He froze as he watched the commotion around us. Then he took a step back. And then another.

He was about to jet.

"Hey!" I shouted. "Wait one second!"

His gaze darted toward me. Then he took off in a run.

I couldn't let him get away!

I darted after him, my muscles straining as I tried to go faster than my body would allow.

Thankfully, Weston saw what was happening, pulled himself away from the gaggle of googly-eyed women around him, and chased after the man.

He caught up with the guy in five seconds flat and tackled him to the ground.

I paused—just slightly—and my eyes widened. So the urban cowboy did have a few real cowboy moves? I was impressed.

Weston sat up and stared the young man in the eye. "What do you think you're doing?"

"Nothing. I'm not doing anything." The teen scrambled back on all fours.

When I reached them, I was breathing entirely more heavily than I would have liked.

I stared at the teen and realized I'd seen him before.

This was the guy who'd been playing the violin on the street corner.

"What's your name?" Weston asked.

"Tommy. I'm Tommy."

"How'd you get that violin, Tommy?" Weston continued. "Were you a part of the scheme to steal it?"

"What? No. It's not like that."

Weston stood and pulled the boy to his feet. "I find that hard to believe. Let's see the violin."

"It's not the one that was stolen, all right?" Tommy raised his hands.

"Then what's in that case?"

He lowered his voice. "It's an imitation. Everyone always says it looks like the real thing. I thought I'd see if I could pass it off for the stolen violin."

"That sounds like a stupid plan," I added.

"It was a stupid plan." Tommy shrugged. "I don't know what to say. I needed the money, and I thought someone might fall for it."

"Why do you need that much money?" I asked.

"Are you the police or something?" Tommy's words came out rapidly as he stared back and forth at Weston and me.

"No, we're not the police." Weston's voice softened. "We're just two people looking for that violin so we can return it to its rightful owner. Now, do you care to keep explaining?"

"I don't know what to say. I'm a street musician, and I need to get my finances in order or find a real job. I've been listening to Dave Ramsey, and he's scared me straight financially."

My eyebrows shot up. I could understand that, I supposed. But his whole line of reasoning didn't make any sense to me.

"You do realize that if the wrong person had shown up, you could have gotten yourself killed, don't you?" Weston beat me to the question.

"I was meeting in public. That's always a good thing, right?"

"You shouldn't get yourself involved with stuff like this," I told him.

"Look, you're sure you don't know anything about the stolen violin?" Weston asked.

"No, I don't know anything. I'm sorry." He raised his hands and took a step back.

"I would suggest you delete that ad you put out there," Weston continued. "Do you understand?"

"Yeah, man, I understand. I'm sorry for all the trouble."

As he walked away, Weston and I exchanged glances. We didn't have to say anything to both feel the other's frustration about that situation.

Tommy could have gotten himself seriously hurt, especially if his plan had worked.

Just as the thought rushed through my head, I looked over and saw a van pull up alongside Tommy. The side door opened, and a man reached out and grabbed him. Just that quick, Tommy was dragged into the van and the vehicle squealed away.

TWENTY-THREE

"HEY! STOP!" I darted after the van, Weston on my heels. But by the time we reached the street it was too late.

I stared at the van as it sped away, trying to see the license plate. But I couldn't read it. The vehicle was too far away.

"The police are on their way." Weston turned back to me as he put his phone away.

"I feel like we should follow after them." I frowned as I watched the van disappear.

"By the time we get back to my truck, they'll be long gone."

I knew his words were true. But I hated feeling so helpless.

Garrison showed up ten minutes later. He jotted notes and sent some officers out to search for the van.

"You have any idea who this guy was?" Garrison asked.

"He said his name was Tommy," I said. "I've actually seen him before. He plays the violin on the corner of River Street. He's probably eighteen or nineteen with light-brown hair that has a touch of curl. He's thin, with a Roman nose and some acne. He was carrying a violin case."

"We'll see what we can find out." Garrison shifted, his expression turning sour. "You should have told me before you came here."

"We didn't know if this was going to go anywhere," I admitted.

A crowd had gathered around us—including that group of women who'd approached Weston earlier. Occasionally, they would add their commentary to the situation or ask for Weston's autograph.

I hadn't seen this side of his life in a long time. Weston handled it well, but the lack of privacy made my anxiety skyrocket.

Garrison locked his gaze with mine. "You could have been the one who was grabbed."

His words made fear shoot through me.

He was right.

That *could* have been me.

In fact, maybe it *should* have been me.

As we climbed back into Weston's truck, I turned to him. "I'm supposed to go have dinner at the Abernathy's. After everything that's happened, I should just cancel."

He let out a breath and shrugged. "I know what you're saying, but there's nothing else you can do to help find Tommy."

I leaned back, his words hitting me like a brick. He was right. But this just felt wrong. "It seems like there should be something else I can do."

"This isn't like some missing couches and tables. I know the police are going to put all their effort into this for now. Let's give them a chance to do their job."

"I guess you're right. Would you come to dinner with me? If I'm going to do this, I don't want to go alone. Not after all this happened."

Weston stared at me a moment and tilted his head. "Are you sure I'm invited?"

"They said I should bring somebody."

"And you didn't ask Zeke?"

Was that jealousy in his voice? I couldn't be sure. "No, I wasn't going to bring anyone. But I would like to bring you."

"Then I'd like to go."

"That sounds great."

We started down the road.

I wished that I felt as peaceful as I might look. But, instead, I felt like the weight of the world was on my shoulders. Was it my fault Tommy had been grabbed?

I knew deep down inside that it wasn't. But if I hadn't asked to meet him . . .

"Don't think like that." Weston's voice cut through the darkness.

I glanced over at him. "How do you know what I'm thinking?"

"Because I can read you like a book. This isn't your fault."

"But I'm the one who set up this meeting . . ."

"Tommy placed the ad. Most likely, these guys were following Tommy, trying to figure out exactly what he did or didn't have. If it hadn't been you meeting him, it would have been someone else."

I let my head fall back against the seat. "I wish I could just let go of it that easily. But I can't."

Weston rubbed his hand across my arm. "I know. All we can do right now is let the police do their job."

I knew he was right and nodded. "I was going to go home and change before I went, but it doesn't look like I'll have time."

"You look like a million bucks. You always do."

I knew that wasn't true. But somehow, Weston made it sound believable.

Now I only hoped my meeting with the Abernathys proved to be fruitful.

TWENTY-FOUR

"I'M SO pleased that you're both here." Mrs. Abernathy clasped her hands in front of her as she grinned, not seeming as icy as she had in the past. "I'm a big fan of yours, Weston Turner."

And *that* was why.

"I'm glad to hear that." Weston flashed his movie star grin. "It's my honor to be here tonight with all of you."

The Abernathys' house was just what I expected —glamorous. Their home was located in an upscale neighborhood and almost looked as if it belonged in Malibu or Palm Springs with its stucco siding and dramatic arches.

Everything about the structure fit the Abernathys.

"I had an interior designer come out and stage the house for us," Mrs. Abernathy explained. "That way we're just 'renting' the furniture until we get ours back—just in case you're wondering."

"I was curious," I admitted.

"Let's not waste any more time. I'm starving." Mrs. Abernathy swept her arm behind her. "Why don't you come have a seat?"

We were ushered to a table that appeared set for royalty with fine china, linens, and an amazing flower centerpiece. Mr. Abernathy and Tara were also there as well as a woman introduced to me as Aunt Beatrice and . . .

Skittles.

My gaze stopped on my assistant as she flashed me a smile.

Wasn't this going to be fun? When Skittles was around, everything was more interesting. She liked it that way.

"I worked for Mr. Abernathy's company last summer," Skittles informed me. "It's because of him I'm the expert filer I am today. I just stopped by for a visit and to talk about more job opportunities. You know what they say: plan for the future or the future will plan you."

I wasn't sure that's what they said at all, but I didn't correct her.

We made general conversation as we ate our salads. Then filet mignon was served, along with roasted fingerling potatoes, blanched green beans, and fresh dinner rolls.

Everything tasted divine—as it should. A professional chef had prepared the meal for us.

As we started the meal, Mr. Abernathy told me about his high-end real estate company in Jacksonville, Florida, and Mrs. Abernathy told me how that had led to them finding this house. Her dream had always been to live here, and Mr. Abernathy finally agreed to commute.

Somewhere along the way, Aunt Beatrice had ended up moving in with them.

It was all very interesting. But what I was most interested in was learning more about that Stradivari.

"So, tell me about your family's history with this violin," I started at a break in the conversation.

"It goes back generations," Mrs. Abernathy said, practically posing with a glass of wine in her hands. "My great-great-grandfather played for the symphony orchestra in Vienna. Someone in each generation has played that Stradivari since then. Until me, of course." She shrugged. "I had no desire."

"Why not?" I carefully cut my steak as I waited for her answer.

"A life in music can consume you." Mrs. Abernathy glanced at me. "I'm sure you know all about that."

"Unfortunately, I do."

"I didn't want that for my future, even if it was my family's legacy."

"But I was hoping to use it," Tara piped in. "I'll begin with the Detroit Symphony Orchestra in another month, and I wanted nothing more than to play an instrument that's been in my family for so long."

"Wouldn't it be a bit of a burden to take care of an instrument that valuable while traveling?" Weston asked. "It seems like you'd always have to be on guard."

"I wouldn't mind." Tara shrugged. "In fact, it would be a privilege. When I think about the places that violin has been, where it's been played, the hands that have touched it . . . it's all worth it."

"That desire obviously skipped a generation with me." Mrs. Abernathy let out a laugh. "I played all throughout college. But when I met Ivan, I knew I was done." She exchanged a look with her husband.

"For the record, I never asked her not to play." Mr. Abernathy leaned back in his seat, listening carefully to the conversation. "That was Barbara's choice."

"I know all about making those choices." I'd

chosen to walk away also. It may have been one of the best decisions I'd ever made for myself.

"Besides, that violin is cursed." Mrs. Abernathy shrugged smugly.

Now she had really had my attention.

"Cursed?" I repeated.

"That's right. Everyone who's ever played it has had bad luck. My great-great-grandfather ended up falling, hitting his head, and dying. My great-grand-father had an aneurism while onstage playing. My grandfather had uncountable tragedies in his life— from divorce to bankruptcy and everything in between. And my own father took his own life before he reached fifty."

"Wow." I shook my head. "I can see where that could be a little strange."

"A little?" Mrs. Abernathy raised her eyebrows. "I've just been waiting for my turn to drop dead."

———

After a successful dinner, Weston and I climbed back into his truck and headed away from the Abernathys.

"You were a hit," I told him.

He shrugged. "Glad I can give people something to talk about."

I grinned then remembered something I needed

to tell him. "By the way, I'm supposed to meet someone about moving some things into my apartment tomorrow."

Weston did a double take at me. "What?"

"I think I found the movers who stole the violin. I called nearly every company I could find until I heard that Boston accent."

Weston did another double take, and his voice rose in pitch. "And you're just now mentioning that?"

I shrugged. "I'm still trying to work out all the details."

"But your stuff is in Atlanta. Where are you going to meet them?"

"I know Atlanta is too far away for me to meet them and come back. I didn't really think things through, I suppose." I let out a long breath. I usually prided myself in being detail-oriented. But my thoughts felt like they were going in a million different directions right now.

"Have them come to my place." Weston's words didn't leave any room for argument. He made it sound like the decision had already been made.

I squinted as I looked over at him. "Your place?"

"Yes, my place. It will be more believable—and doable."

I let out a hesitant breath. "But I've already talked

to these guys. What sense would it make for them to show up somewhere I don't live?"

"We can tell them we're together, that we're getting married and that I need to move my stuff to your place. We'll come up with some type of cover story. But you can't do this alone or in Atlanta."

"I don't want to put you in the middle of this either. Especially after Tommy . . ." I shuddered as I remembered everything that had just happened.

"I'd much rather be in the middle of this than have you do it alone." Weston glanced at me again. "Listen, how about we stop by the police station to see if Garrison has anything to tell us about Tommy?"

I nodded. "That sounds like a great idea."

"I'll drive you to the station . . . as long as you agree that, when you call these movers back, you'll make it seem as if I'm the one who's moving and not you."

That sounded doable enough—although I'd totally noticed what he did. "It's a deal."

"Okay then. Let's go." Weston took a left turn and headed toward the station.

CHAPTER
TWENTY-FIVE

"YOU KNOW I can't share that kind of information with you." Garrison crossed his arms as he leaned back in his seat at his desk.

His words hadn't surprised me. In fact, they were exactly what I'd expected.

"Can you just tell us if you found him?" Weston shifted as we stood in front of the detective.

Garrison frowned and looked around before turning back to us. Then he lowered his voice, almost as if his earlier statement had just been for the sake of putting on a show and for plausible deniability.

"No, not yet," he said quietly. "But I do have a name for you. This guy is Tommy Gleason. He's nineteen. He lives with five other guys in an apartment not far from downtown."

"Five other guys?" I repeated.

"They all work low-paying jobs to try to make ends meet. Tommy makes his money by playing on the street corner. Apparently, it's a decent gig. He's never missed a month's rent, but he doesn't have much left over either."

"Can you tell us anything else?" Weston asked.

Garrison let out a long breath. "Seems like Tommy's a good kid. We're still trying to get in touch with his parents. They live up in Fayetteville, apparently."

I sighed and rubbed my arms as I imagined his parents getting that call. Their whole lives would be turned upside down. I lifted a prayer for them.

"I just don't understand why anyone would grab Tommy," I muttered.

"The only thing I can think of is that maybe someone saw the ad and thought Tommy had the violin. They realized how valuable the instrument was and wanted it for themselves."

Some kind of memory kept trying to whisper itself into my ear. It had to do with Tommy's abduction . . .

"What is it, Camryn?" Garrison stared at me.

I ran a hand across my forehead wishing I could assemble my thoughts as easily as putting together a casserole.

It was a sound that begged for my attention . . .

something I hadn't even realized that I'd heard.

Then it hit me . . . "I know this is going to sound weird, but something seemed familiar about how the van's engine sounded."

Garrison stared at me, something close to a dumbfounded expression on his face. "You're telling me that motors sound different on different vehicles and that you can tell the difference?"

I narrowed my eyes and nodded, not excited or impressed at the admission—it actually felt like a big responsibility. "Believe me, I wish that I didn't. But there are different nuances to every type of machine that runs. And something about the van as it squealed away sounded like I'd heard it before."

"So, you think you've seen the van before?" Weston turned toward me. "Wouldn't you remember that?"

I shook my head, still trying to get the pieces to fall into place. "I don't know. I feel like my brain is trying to make the connection, but it's not quite there yet."

"Take a few minutes if you need to," Garrison said.

I rubbed my temples again, trying to clear away all the other noise in the room. But it was no use. This place was busy. Every sound cut into my thoughts—people talking, phones ringing, doors opening.

Weston handed me some noise canceling earbuds. "Try these."

I offered a grateful smile. "Good idea."

I slipped them into my ears and pressed a button on the side of the earbuds.

The noise around me disappeared.

Sucking in a deep breath, I closed my eyes and tried to rewind time in my mind.

I wasn't exaggerating this. I'd heard the sound of that engine before.

But where?

I was pretty sure I'd heard it recently.

I continued rewinding in my mind the events of the past several days.

Until finally I stopped at one place.

I raised my head and opened my eyes, pulling out the earbuds and grasping them in my hands.

"Where did you hear it?" Garrison peered at me as if anticipating my answer.

My gaze locked with his. "Blue's Garage. The mechanics were working on it outside behind the building when we were there. I didn't see the van. I only heard it."

"Are you sure?" Garrison asked.

I nodded. "I'm sure."

Garrison grabbed his keys from his pocket and stepped toward the door. "Let's go."

TWENTY-SIX

"I DON'T KNOW what you're talking about." Carl stood in the car bay at Blue's and stared at Detective Garrison, an edge creeping into his voice. "I didn't kidnap some teenager, and I don't own a van."

"Were you working on a white van earlier this week?" Garrison looked unaffected by Carl's defensiveness.

For some reason, the detective had let Weston and me accompany him and his partner to Blue's Garage—as long as we stayed out of their way. We'd agreed.

"We work on a lot of vehicles." Carl sounded much less genteel this time than when I'd first met him.

He was really feeling threatened right now, wasn't he?

"You're going to need to think a little bit harder

about this." Garrison's voice hardened as if to let Carl know he meant business.

Carl let out a sigh as he furiously wiped his grease-stained hands on a dirty rag. "Yes, I think I remember working on the white van. But I don't know who it belongs to, and it's definitely not mine."

"Can you look at your records and see who owns it then?" Garrison tapped his foot as if getting annoyed.

Carl's gaze locked with Garrison's. "Do you have a warrant?"

Garrison stepped closer and narrowed his eyes. "Do you really want to stand in the way of a missing persons investigation? Especially when you're the prime suspect."

Carl backed toward the office, fear washing through his gaze as he raised his hands in the air. "Okay. Okay. I get it. I just don't want any trouble."

Garrison followed him into the office.

"Do you think he's going to turn over the information?" I whispered to Weston as we remained where we were. There wasn't enough room in the office for all five of us.

"If Carl knows what's best for him, he's going to cooperate."

A moment later, Garrison emerged with a paper in his hand. He raised it in the air as he said, "We have a name and a VIN number. Now, let's see what we can find out."

Hope stirred in my heart.

Maybe we'd find Tommy, and he would be okay.

That was my prayer.

———

When I got back to the apartment, Zeke was waiting inside for me. I'd given him a key.

In fact, he wasn't *just* inside.

He was waiting at the door, almost like a father waiting for a daughter to return home from her first date.

As I lingered in the doorway, Weston and Zeke stared at each other for several moments. Finally, I cleared my throat, hating the tension tugging at the air right now.

"Weston and I got caught up in some things," I explained to Zeke. "I'll tell you all about them."

Weston stepped back, his gaze darkening. But clearly, he had no reason to feel territorial over me. Neither did Zeke, for that matter.

"I'll get going," Weston said. "But call me if you hear anything."

"If you hear anything?" Zeke repeated.

He wasn't going to be happy with all that happened, was he?

But I could make my own decisions, and no amount of chiding was going to change that.

"I'll fill you in," I told him.

I cast another smile at Weston before slipping into my apartment and closing the door.

As we sat in the living room, I updated Zeke on tonight's turn of events.

Just as he started to ask a question, my phone buzzed.

Garrison had texted me:

The van was stolen.

I fought disappointment as I read his words. Stolen?

Did that mean that all our work tonight had led us nowhere?

That's how it appeared.

My lungs deflated at the thought.

And what about Tommy?

I told Zeke the news.

Zeke shifted on the couch. "I'm sorry to hear that. But I do have a surprise for you. Maybe it will cheer you up a bit and distract you from everything else."

I turned toward him, trying to turn my thoughts from the mystery. "What's that?"

He reached behind the kitchen counter and held up a bag. "Christmas decorations. I wasn't sure where yours were—and I didn't want to snoop—so I picked up a few things while I was in town."

"What?" I'd already pulled my own out once. That was when I found the jump drive. Finding that had derailed me, and I'd abandoned any decorating I'd been attempting.

Zeke shrugged. "I can't let you celebrate Christmas without your tree having any ornaments."

I started to argue when I realized his actions were actually very thoughtful. "You didn't have to do that . . ."

"I know. I wanted to. I hope I didn't overstep." He shrugged as he waited for my response.

Had he? I wasn't sure.

But I felt certain Zeke's intentions were good.

I forced a smile. "You didn't overstep. Not at all."

An hour later, the tree was up, the lights put on, and garland stretched between the branches. We drank peppermint hot chocolate and ate some popcorn, making the moment somewhat of a cele-bration.

We were now hanging the last few ornaments and

listening to one of Amy Grant's Christmas albums. They'd always been my favorite.

As I reached to put an ornament on a top branch, my arm brushed with Zeke's, and I paused. My first impulse was to apologize and step away.

Instead, our gazes caught.

Something passed between us—something that made my throat go dry.

As "Tennessee Christmas" crooned in the background, he stepped closer.

My heart pounded harder as my thoughts raced.

Zeke was handsome. Successful. A good person. He'd proven himself to be a good friend time and time again.

Could there be something more between us?

His gaze swept to my lips, and he leaned closer. Wrapped an arm around my waist.

The next instant, our lips met.

The moment they did, I popped away from him.

Guilt flooded me.

I couldn't kiss someone else.

I was married to . . . Phil.

Except I wasn't.

My hand rushed over my lips as my thoughts continued to race.

"I'm sorry." Zeke stepped away, his hand dropping from my waist. "I shouldn't have done that. I don't know what I was thinking."

"No . . . it's okay. I just . . ." I just what? I wasn't sure.

"I thought there could be something between us."

"I felt it too," I told him. "But Phil . . ."

"You don't have to explain." He raised a hand to stop me. "I just thought . . ."

I rubbed my lips, trying to get my thoughts under control. "It's just . . . I haven't . . . kissed anyone since—"

Zeke squeezed my arm. "Maybe we should forget that ever happened."

As apprehension pounded inside me, I nodded. "Maybe."

But was that really what I wanted?

I wasn't sure right now.

Instead of continuing this awkward conversation, I pointed over my shoulder. "I think maybe I should go to bed. It's been a long day."

Zeke stared at me, turbulent emotions thrashing in his gaze. "I understand. Good night, Camryn. I'll clean up in here."

"Good night." Then I fled to my bedroom so I could process what had just happened and all the feelings that went with it.

TWENTY-SEVEN

AT SEVEN THE NEXT MORNING, Weston picked me up so we could arrange things at his house for our possible meeting with the movers tonight. We wanted to start on it early to make it to work on time.

Weston had coffee waiting for me in the truck, fixed just the way I liked it, which gave him major bonus points.

Zeke had already left for his meeting with one of his former employees who'd worked with Phil at Bromtech.

Zeke . . .

I'd thought about our kiss all night. One minute, I was glad it happened. The next, I regretted it.

Even after a fitful night of sleep, I still didn't

know what to think about it. My attempt to rest hadn't given me any clarity.

I was just glad that I didn't have to be around Zeke for any extended period of time today. I was certain things would be awkward between us, and awkward wasn't my favorite emotion.

I also couldn't stop thinking about Tommy. I wondered if there were any updates. I prayed he was okay. I'd prayed that for the teen all night.

I couldn't help but think it was somehow my fault, even though he was the one who'd placed the ad in the magazine.

Finally, we arrived at Weston's place and he ushered me inside.

I stood in the living room and glanced around. This was the first time I'd been there.

The place was smaller than I'd expected, especially considering Weston's success. It was humble and modest—I liked that. I'd halfway expected a professional designer to have helped him, but from the looks of it, he'd decorated this place himself.

Awards, as well as three guitars, were displayed on the wall behind the couch. Several plants were scattered throughout the space—all of them alive. An accent wall was painted cobalt blue.

"I like it." I nodded with approval.

"It's home."

I turned toward Weston, wondering if he'd had any second thoughts about our plan for the day. "Are you sure you're up for this?"

He stared at me, his gaze showing no signs of hesitation. "I'm up for it if you are."

I knew what he was really saying. He meant that if I was going to be involved with this shenanigan, then so was he.

The realization warmed my heart.

But I cleared those thoughts from my head, and I held up some tracking chips I'd purchased. "So, these have stickers on the back. We can strategically place them and then follow your furniture as it's moved."

Weston took one from me, our fingers brushing as he studied it. His cowboy attire—chambray shirt, fitted jeans, and cowboy boots—painted quite the picture.

They always did.

He glanced back up at me. "Are you sure these are going to work?"

"Am I sure? Not a hundred percent. That's why I purchased more than one, just in case. I'm also thinking we don't need to have all your items moved. Maybe we can tell the movers that some items are going to be sold and that way they're only taking a few things. I mean, I think we're going to get your items back. But what if we don't?"

Worst-case scenarios began rushing through my head, and panic rose so quickly I felt strangled.

Weston's hand came down on my shoulder. "It's going to be okay. You know how I am. Stuff is just stuff. None of this means anything to me." He swept his other hand out to display the room.

I pointed to one of his guitars. "Not even that?"

He glanced at them. "I do love my guitars. But it's not like I can take them with me one day."

"But there is sentimental value in them—kind of like the Abernathys' violin. With history comes memories—and memories are precious."

"I suppose there is that." Weston shrugged, still looking unconvinced.

I took another sip of my coffee, knowing the caffeine wasn't good for my nerves.

"Let's get this done," I finally said.

We wandered through Weston's house and strategically picked several items to be moved—a chair, a couple of tables, a houseplant, a bookcase, a spare bed, and a dresser.

"Something about you seems different," Weston said as I stuck a tracker beneath an end table. "I've been noticing it all morning."

I'd felt him observing me as I worked.

I shrugged, pushing aside thoughts about the kiss

that Zeke and I had shared. That was definitely not something I wanted to confide to Weston about.

Instead, I said, "There's a lot on my mind, I suppose."

"How long is Zeke going to be in town?"

I frowned. It was almost as if Weston knew the two of us had kissed—or at least he suspected it.

Was I that obvious?

Maybe not to most people. But possibly to Weston.

"I'm not sure," I told him.

Before we could talk anymore, Weston's phone rang, and he stepped toward the bedrooms. I could tell by the way his voice rose that the discussion wasn't good, but I tried my best not to listen.

Despite that, it sounded like Weston had some issues of his own.

He returned a moment later.

"That was Athena. You know how that goes." His eyes rolled to the side as if he tried to restrain his irritation but failed.

"Are you guys still trying to figure out the custody?"

He let out a long sigh as he lifted his hat and raked his hand through his hair. "Honestly, she's dating a new guy, and he might be moving in with her. I don't approve. I don't want this guy around my kids."

"Why not?"

"He's trouble. He has a history with drugs and violence. But I guess he's living up to the bad boy vibe she's looking for right now." He scowled as he ended his statement.

My heart panged with compassion for him. But I knew there was nothing I could say that would make it better. "I'm sorry to hear that. I can only imagine how difficult that would be. I don't suppose you have any say in the situation?"

"Not legally. He's Pete Hedgesworth." His lips flickered down in a frown.

Pete Hedgesworth? The rock 'n' roll guy? Even I knew he was trouble. I'd run into him once at an award show, and he'd hit on me—even though he was dating someone else. That wasn't even to mention the fact that he was daily tabloid fodder for his arrests and bad behavior.

No mother in her right mind would expose her kids to that kind of person—in my opinion, at least.

"I'll be praying for you." I wished there was more I could do—but there wasn't. However, there was power in prayer.

"I can use all the prayers I can get." Weston pressed his lips together in a grim line.

I could tell this was bothering him—as it should.

He let out a long breath and glanced around his living room, as if turning his thoughts from his troubles to our current project. "Let's get finished here. Then I guess we need to get to work."

I wanted to argue or to find another excuse to talk about this more. But I couldn't. Weston was right. We did have a lot to do at work—including finalizing last-minute details for The Christmas Thing.

I stuck one more tracker into a plant. I'd put out six of them altogether. Then I pulled up my phone to make sure the locations showed up on the app.

They did.

I only hoped that we weren't going through all of this trouble for nothing.

But that remained to be seen.

———

As Weston drove us to Grand Isle, Garrison called.

My breath caught as hope sprang inside me. Maybe there would be an update. I hadn't been able to stop thinking about Tommy.

I put the detective on speaker so Weston could also hear.

"We found Tommy this morning." Garrison got right to the point.

I swallowed hard. His clipped tone didn't indicate a happy ending.

"And?" I asked.

"He's alive but pretty beaten up. It looks like these guys shoved him from the van onto the side of the road. Another car didn't see him there and hit him. He's in critical condition."

I pressed my eyes closed. "I'm so sorry to hear that."

"We all are. He's not able to talk to us, or anyone, right now. I thought you would want to know."

"Thanks so much for the update." I ended the call, lowered my phone, and glanced at Weston. "That certainly wasn't what I wanted to hear."

Weston frowned as he gripped the steering wheel. "Me neither. I hope he pulls through."

"This whole investigation just keeps getting stranger and stranger."

"You can say that again."

We pulled up at the school, but instead of getting out of his truck, Weston turned toward me. "Rehearsal at noon and then tonight at my place at six to meet the movers, right?"

My day was shaping up to be quite busy. "That's the plan."

He nodded, something lingering in his gaze. "Sounds good."

I knew there was more on his mind than that.

I turned to face him. "What are you thinking?"

He touched the brim of his hat and readjusted it slightly. "Listen . . . have you thought about our duet anymore? If we're going to do it, we'll need to practice."

"You don't think it's like riding a bike—that we'll just remember?"

His gaze caught mine. "I know you. You love rehearsing."

I smiled. He remembered that. "I do. I'll let you know soon. I promise."

He nodded. "Okay. Now, let's just hope none of the students saw us riding together this morning. That's a definite way to start the rumor mill going."

"Yes, it is. I'll get out first. You trail behind me in a couple of minutes, okay?"

He grinned and winked. "Got it. It will be like the old days when we tried to keep our relationship under wraps."

Memories filled my soul almost like a sweet song sweeping me back in time. But I didn't want to embrace those feelings. There was too much on the line right now.

Instead, I nodded and slipped from his truck.

I had other things I needed to think about . . . if I were wise.

TWENTY-EIGHT

FOR THE REST of the morning, I sat at my desk, trying to forget about Tommy and the missing violin and any trouble Phil had gotten caught up in.

Instead, I worked on my obligations here at the conservatory. I even closed my office door so no one would disturb me.

At eleven, Mrs. Abernathy called.

I was surprised when she announced, "I have a lead."

I straightened in my chair. "A lead?"

"Yes, a man named Felix Gildersleeve. You ever heard of him?"

As a matter of fact, I had heard of him. "The symphony conductor, right?"

"Yes, he's the one. Anyway, he's been interested

in my violin for years, but we've always told him we weren't interested in selling."

"Okay . . ." I was curious to hear where she was going with this.

"It turns out he lives here in Savannah—he keeps that fact private, however. We have a mutual friend, and he told us that Gildersleeve was asking about our move and that he sounded overly curious about all the details. He even mentioned the violin."

I paused, letting that sink in. "Really . . ."

"I think he should be questioned."

"You think he hired these guys to steal it?"

"It's my best guess. Gildersleeve is a collector. He always gets what he wants."

"I'll see what I can do."

"I know you will. Thanks, dear."

I know you will? Something about the way Mrs. Abernathy said the words made it sound like she was the one calling the shots. I wasn't sure how I felt about that. How I proceeded was up to *me*.

But I also knew this was one lead I couldn't walk away from.

Felix Gildersleeve had a reputation as being immensely talented but exceedingly horrible to work with. He was smart, but he thought highly of himself —too highly. I wouldn't put it past someone that narcissistic to do something like this.

The only reason I knew that was because one of my old friends had played viola for him for a year, and she'd often moaned about how pompous and difficult he was.

How would I get in touch with him?

Would I even have time to pursue this lead today?

I glanced at my watch and saw it was almost noon.

Right now, I had to get to rehearsal.

———

As the rehearsal ended and we were cleaning up, someone stepped through the doors at the back of the auditorium and strode toward the stage.

Professor Amile.

And his gaze was on me as I stood by the orchestra pit discussing details with our stage manager. As he approached, I dismissed her so I could see what Amile wanted. He'd obviously come here with a purpose.

I lowered my clipboard to my side as I turned toward him. "Professor . . . what brings you here?"

As the band on stage played a few more strands of "God Rest Ye Merry, Gentlemen," Amile cleared his throat and tugged on the lapels of his tweed suit-coat—complete with elbow patches.

"Good evening, Mrs. Paine," he began. "I hope you don't mind me stopping by, but I've been curious ever since the two of us talked. I wondered if there were any updates on the Stradivari."

I shook my head, feeling an unseen pressure push into me at the question. It was a reminder of how little progress I'd made.

"I wish there was," I told him. "But, unfortunately, no. We've only hit dead ends."

He puckered his lips in disappointment. "That's too bad—but not surprising."

Ouch. He'd had no faith in me.

But I wouldn't let it bother me. I knew what I was up against, even if he didn't.

"The good thing is that the FBI is involved," I told him. "Maybe they'll have more success."

"The feds are investigating?" His eyebrows shot up. "I'm surprised they haven't called me. I've been consulted for the Art Loss Register and Art Recovery International on more than one occasion. I'm pretty good at what I do."

I leaned against the railing lining the orchestra pit, wondering if this man had shown up just to insult me and exalt himself. That's how it seemed.

"Is there anything you would tell them that you haven't told me?" I figured I might as well put the question out there.

Amile let out a chuckle. "It depends on what questions they ask. But overall—no. I told you what I know. I've been keeping my ears open for any updates from auction houses, but I haven't heard anything."

That was disappointing, but then again—what had I expected?

"I hope the violin turns up," I told him. "It would be a shame for an instrument like that to disappear forever."

He let out a harsh chuckle. "Someone isn't going to hold onto an instrument like that—not if they know they can sell it and make millions."

"True." Money was a great motivator for many people.

Amile let out a sigh before taking a step back. "If I hear anything, I'll let you know."

"I appreciate it."

As he walked away, Weston joined me, and we watched the professor walk out the back door.

"Amile actually took the initiative to talk to you," Weston murmured. "That's pretty amazing."

"What do you mean?" I glanced up at him as I pondered his words.

"I mean, Amile usually keeps to himself. He only talks when he's asked a question. He defines intro-vert to a T."

"Interesting. He seems invested in this missing Stradivari."

"I guess anyone will talk if the subject interests them enough."

I only wished I could figure out a way to find out the information I needed from Amile—or from anyone, for that matter.

Even though investigating seemed to ignite something inside me, maybe I should leave it to the professionals. My ear for detail didn't seem to be getting me anywhere—and I didn't see that changing in the future.

CHAPTER
TWENTY-NINE

THAT EVENING, as the sun sank below the horizon, I frowned as I stood in Weston's front yard and watched the movers carry items from his home into a white moving truck with a dented door.

These weren't the same men from the videos I'd obtained from the other crimes. I was certain of it.

Had this whole charade been for nothing?

That's how it appeared.

More discouragement pressed on me.

"Congrats on the upcoming wedding," one of the movers called as he walked by carrying a box of books.

The man was probably in his twenties, with dark hair, a scraggly beard, and an uneven smile.

Again—I'd never seen him before.

Weston reached for my hand—only because we

were pretending to be together, of course. "Thank you. We're super excited. Aren't we, snookums?"

"So excited." I raised my shoulders and tilted my head as if I were giddy. Weston really was laying it on thick, wasn't he?

"You two look happy together."

I swung my hand—the one holding Weston's—and grinned. "We are. He's the best thing that ever happened to me—and I've had a lot of great things happen to me."

I swallowed hard after the words left my lips.

I was just acting . . . right?

Then why did something about my words sound almost real?

The man nodded at us. "I wish you two the best."

Weston and I exchanged a cheesy, over-the-moon grin—just like any good, in-love couple would.

I watched as the men disappeared back inside the house again.

"Camryn?" Weston moved close and slipped his arm around my waist. "What are you thinking?"

I let out a sigh. "These aren't the right people, Weston. When I talked to the guy on the phone, he had a Boston accent. These people aren't the ones from the video. It doesn't make sense that whoever is behind this would pull in new people. It would just increase the possibilities that someone might sell them out."

"Unless the guy behind this is trying to hide his previous involvement. He could have hired all new people, and they could all be clueless about what's going on." He shrugged, not pushing his theory but simply putting it out there.

I stared at two men as they carried a dresser through Weston's front door.

He could be right.

After the team moved the big items we'd requested them to transport, the lead guy paused in front of us. "I'm sure it was explained to you that we wouldn't be able to drop these off tonight, right?"

"That's correct," Weston answered.

"It was too much of a last-minute job, and my guys want to get home to their families. So, we'll drop these items by your new place in the morning."

"What time?" Weston asked. "I want to make sure I can be there."

The man looked at the clipboard he held. "It's scheduled for nine a.m. Does that work?"

Weston flashed a smile. "That sounds perfect."

As I watched them drive away, I prayed Weston and I knew what we were doing.

I was trying to put all the right safety precautions in place . . . but what if I failed?

"Where are they now?" Weston peered toward me as he looked at my phone.

We sat beside each other on his couch. We might as well be watching a football game or a concert. We were that invested in watching this play out.

We'd also ordered Chinese food. My container of beef and broccoli sat on the table in front of me. Weston was eating orange chicken.

"They're driving north on the highway," I told him. "If this was a legit company, where would they park the truck overnight?"

"I'm guessing somewhere gated."

My heart thrummed in my ears as I continued to watch the moving icon on my screen. "Should we follow them?"

"I think we should watch where they go. Maybe once they stop, we can get the police involved. We definitely shouldn't try to confront them ourselves."

"I agree."

Neither Weston nor I had any kind of law enforcement experience. We had to be smart here. I needed to remember that and not let my emotions get the best of me.

"Okay, while we wait, maybe we should look up

everything we can find on Gildersleeve." I picked up my container of food.

"Gildersleeve?"

I grabbed a piece of beef with my chopsticks. "Sorry—I thought I'd told you. Felix Gildersleeve is a symphony conductor who collects antique instruments. He's been wanting to purchase the Stradivari from the Abernathys for a while, but they've refused."

Weston scooped up some fried rice and paused with it. "So, you think he put these guys up to stealing it? Sounds extreme. What good is it to own a fantastic instrument if you can't brag about it?"

"I get where you're coming from. But maybe this guy finds pleasure in the hunt of it all. Not everyone wants to show off what they have."

Weston nodded. "You're right. But I'm sure he's not going to easily volunteer any of this information."

"I agree. I've been thinking about it. Maybe we can approach him from the standpoint of the school. No one really knows I'm investigating, after all."

He raised an eyebrow. "No one?"

He had me there. "Well, no one but the Abernathys, Skittles, Hannon, the Whitmores—"

"And all the other people you've already talked to." Weston gave me a pointed look. "If someone is keeping an eye on this case, then they definitely know you're involved."

I shrugged and grabbed a piece of broccoli this time. I was hungrier than I'd thought. "I still think we should talk to him."

He stared at me a moment—and I waited for a lecture.

Instead, he nodded. "Then go for it. If you want me to go with you, I'd be happy to. I just don't want you to go alone."

I heard the concern in his voice—and the earnestness. "I appreciate that. Thank you."

We stared at each other a moment before Weston looked away and let out a sigh. "Just remember that dress rehearsal is in two days, and the performance is only three days away."

"I know. It's hard to believe. Then Winter Break will officially begin."

There was a time in my life when those words would have excited me. But no more. In fact, I'd almost rather stay here and work, to keep busy rather than think about what I'd lost.

I needed to turn that around. Instead, I needed to think about what I'd gained.

A new job. New friends. New adventures.

Keeping that at the forefront of my thoughts was going to require some effort, however.

"We might need to look into Gildersleeve some other time." Weston's voice brought me back from my thoughts. "Camryn. Look."

He pointed to my cell phone screen.

My breath caught.

Weston was right.

We had more pressing matters to attend to.

CHAPTER
THIRTY

I LEANED back on Weston's couch and stared at my phone. I couldn't seem to take my eyes off it.

Even after Weston brought me some peppermint hot chocolate, I was only distracted a moment. Even when Weston sat down only inches from me so he could also see my phone, that only distracted me for a moment also.

Okay, maybe a little bit longer. Especially when I smelled his leather aftershave and my mind tried to transport me back in time.

Another lifetime ago, I would have leaned into him. He would have put his arms around me. We would have talked about our future. About music. About how we could conquer the world.

How things had changed.

I frowned at the thought.

I took another sip of the hot chocolate and stared at the map on my screen. "This must be where these guys took the truck for the night. They haven't moved in an hour."

Weston leaned closer. "But it looks like they're in the middle of nowhere."

I let out a sigh. I couldn't deny his words. Based on what I saw on this map, the moving truck was on the side of the road in the boondocks.

Why would they do that?

"What do you think we should do?" I looked up at Weston hoping he had a suggestion because I was running out of ideas.

He rubbed a hand across his beard before shaking his head. "Maybe we could drive past. I don't want to alert the police for no reason. I don't want to be like the girl who cried wolf. But if something's happening right now that could lead us to an arrest, I don't want to ignore that either."

I stood. I'd been hoping he'd say that. "Then let's go."

He let out a chuckle. "It's nice to see you so enthusiastic."

I reached out my hand to help him up also. As our fingers touched, I felt a spark of electricity shoot through me.

I quickly let go.

This was no time to be feeling sparks.

I'd already kissed my husband's best friend. My life was complicated enough without adding more confusion to the mix.

I ran my hand down my jeans and forced a smile, hoping I still looked composed. "I'm ready when you are."

Weston placed his hand on the small of my back and led me to the door. A few minutes later, we were heading down the road.

"Listen, I'm sorry to hear about everything you're going through right now—with Phil and such," he started, a frown tugging at his lips. "I can only imagine how rough that might be."

At the mention of Phil, my heart grew heavier. "It's been a bit overwhelming, to say the least."

"Have there been any updates?"

"I know Zeke's been looking into some things. But I still don't think we're any closer to answers than we were before."

"That's too bad. If there's anything I can do to help . . ."

I offered a grateful smile. "You're already doing plenty. Thank you. You've been a great sport about all of this."

"It's no problem. I know it's been frustrating for you."

"It sure has. If there's one thing I hate, it's leaving things unresolved. Having both of these cases hanging over me is enough to drive me crazy."

"In a few days, The Christmas Thing will be over, so at least that will be one less action item on your mind."

"Then before we know it, it will be Christmas."

Silence fell in the truck at my words. Weston and I both knew that Christmas wouldn't be the same this year. We'd already talked about it so there was no need to rehash it anymore.

But I had times when I wondered why things had to change. I wished I could bottle the sweet moments in life and repeat them over and over. Then I also wished I could bottle the bad moments and throw them into a deep hole where no one would ever find them.

Unfortunately, life didn't work like that.

I glanced at the tracker app on my phone and saw we were getting closer.

A couple of minutes later, the icon indicated we were on top of the moving truck.

Problem was that there was no truck in sight— Weston and I were on a country road with nothing around us except old cotton fields and enormous ditches.

———

Weston pulled his truck over, and we stood on the side of the road. I tugged my coat closer to ward off a chilly wind that swept over the open field around us. Without any streetlights, it was dark out here. Really dark.

"I don't understand . . ." I muttered as I glanced around at the nothingness surrounding us. There wasn't even a tree or a barn nearby to hide a truck behind.

Weston shrugged. "Maybe those trackers aren't as great as the reviews said."

I kicked a rock at my feet and sighed. "Do you think they drove this way and the trackers all suddenly died at the same time?"

"It's doubtful." He glanced at the ground, and, the next moment, he hopped across the ditch and bent down.

I leaned closer as I tried to figure out what he was doing. "Do you see something?"

He grabbed a stick and extended it into the grassy trench. A few minutes later, he scraped something from the edge.

I let out a long breath when I saw what the object was.

A tracker . . .

"They must have discovered we planted those on the furniture," Weston said.

"But how? And how did they find all of them if that's the case?"

"Maybe there's some type of technology that would help them do this. I'm not sure. Maybe it's just part of their protocol."

I crossed my arms and shook my head. I found that hard to believe.

"So, I guess we just went through all this trouble for nothing," I said with resignation. "Your furniture . . ."

Weston rose to his feet. "I'm sure I can get it back. For a price."

"Oh, Weston . . ." Regret pounded inside me.

He hopped back to this side of the ditch and stood in front of me, the moonlight glinting on his hair. "It's okay, Camryn. I promise you, it's okay."

But it didn't feel okay.

I should have never agreed to take this case. I should have backed off and let the police handle it. Every lead I pursued only seemed to lead to trouble.

I stared at the tracker one more time. "I think this

is the part where I need to call Garrison and let him know what's going on."

Weston frowned. "I know this isn't what you wanted, but calling Garrison is probably a good idea."

CHAPTER
THIRTY-ONE

WESTON WALKED me up to my apartment, said good night, and then I stepped inside, knowing that Zeke was there. He'd texted me earlier to ask how I was doing.

Part of me dreaded seeing him right now.

Part of me looked forward to it.

Either way, I was an adult so I could handle this like an adult.

Zeke stiffly rose to his feet when he saw me. "Camryn . . . how did everything go?"

I deposited my purse onto a table in the foyer then took my coat off and hung it near the door. "Not exactly as I planned."

I explained to him what happened, and he frowned.

"I wish you'd waited for me," he said.

"I know . . . but I was trying to strike while the iron was hot, as the saying goes."

"It was a valiant effort." He offered a weak smile.

"Thanks." But I didn't feel like I deserved any pats on the back. The only thing I had succeeded in doing was losing Weston's belongings.

I knew I should have used my own. But it was too late to go back.

I shifted as I stood in the living room, wishing things felt normal between us again. Hopefully, with some time. "Anything new with you? Any updates that you're able to share?"

Zeke shook his head. "I'm not getting anywhere asking questions. I don't want to show my hand and let these guys know that I know what's going on. But, clearly, they already suspect that I know something. Either way, without any more concrete evidence to give me direction as to where to look, I almost feel like I'm at a standstill also."

I frowned and rubbed my arms. "I'm sorry. I know that's frustrating."

"It is."

"How was your meeting with your employee who worked the case with Phil?" I rushed.

Zeke let out a sigh. "I was hoping he had some information. But you know Phil. He was tight-lipped. You could trust him with your secrets—which was a good thing as a friend but not so great during an investigation."

I frowned. I couldn't argue with his assessment. It was completely accurate.

Zeke paused and looked at me another moment. "Camryn, about that kiss . . ."

I raised my hand. "There's really nothing else to say about it. Why don't we just pretend that it didn't happen, like you suggested?"

He stepped closer to me. "There's a part of me that doesn't want to pretend it didn't happen."

I swallowed a lump in my throat. "I understand, it's just that . . ."

"Phil," he answered with a frown.

I nodded and dragged my gaze back up to meet his. "It's strange. It feels wrong even if it isn't."

Zeke started to reach out to touch my arm, but he dropped his hand back to his side instead. "I get it. I just don't want things to be weird between us."

"I know. That's why I said let's pretend it didn't happen. Deal?"

He grinned. "Deal—for now, at least."

I nodded down the hallway. "It's been a long day, so I think I'm going to get some sleep."

He stared at me another moment as if he wanted to say more. "Good night, Camryn."

"Good night, Zeke."

I only wish that pretending that kiss never happened was a legitimate option.

Because I actually couldn't stop thinking about it.

———

The next morning, I went to talk to Felix Gildersleeve. I'd quickly researched the man before I left, trying to find anything that could be useful. Mostly, I'd just found his awards and accolades, however.

My friend and Grand Isle voice professor, Jinky Jennings, had agreed to come with me.

Jinky had a larger-than-life personality and the looks to go with it. Big, blonde hair and blue eyes accentuated by her colorful eyeshadow. Bright clothing that drew attention to her along with a loud laugh and an effervescent smile.

The two of us had been friends all throughout college, and, although we had lost touch afterward, we picked up where we left off when I came back to Grand Isle. She'd invited me over for dinner with her and her husband on several occasions, and the two of us had even gone Christmas shopping together a couple of times already.

"I get to help with one of your investigations." She barely subdued a squeal. "I am so excited."

"Thanks for coming along with me." I knew I couldn't go alone, and I didn't want to ask Zeke to come with me. Besides, he was back at Bromtech again. I knew that Weston had a class this morning. That left either Skittles or Jinky.

I picked Jinky.

We pulled to a stop in front of Felix Gildersleeve's house, and I stared up at the massive place.

I had lived in Nashville for a while, so I was accustomed to large homes. But this one certainly was grand and stately with its deep-red bricks, black shutters, and colonial styling.

As we climbed from Jinky's car and began to walk toward the door, Jinky turned to me. "If I actually meet Felix Gildersleeve, it will be the most amazing thing to happen to me this year. He does know we're coming, right?"

I nibbled on my lip before shrugging. "Not really."

"What do you mean *not really*? That doesn't even sound like you."

"I mean, I called, but he didn't answer. So now I have to resort to other means."

"Oh." Her smile fell a little bit.

"What? I left him a voice mail."

"Oh, that makes it okay then," Jinky said but didn't sound convinced.

"We've got this," I insisted. I was the type who liked to think things through and have a plan. But, sometimes, I had to let go of that tendency and just go with the flow.

Three years ago, I wouldn't have been able to do this. But losing Phil had reminded me of how short life is. I had to take risks sometimes.

That's what I was doing right now.

I took the lead and charged toward the front door. A moment of self-doubt hit me right as I rang the bell, but I ignored it. If this was a train wreck, then there was nothing I could do to stop it now. It would take entirely too long for the brakes to kick in.

The doorbell rang, playing Mozart's "Eine kleine Nachtmusik," the chimes sounding real, as if they'd been buried within the walls of the entryway.

A moment later, a man answered the door—a man who was not Felix Gildersleeve. The slight man wore a black suit and a snooty expression.

Did Gildersleeve actually have a butler? It appeared so.

"Can I help you?" the man asked, his accent distinctly British.

"Hello." I put on my most charming smile. "I'm Camryn Paine, and this is my friend, Jinky Jennings. We're with Grand Isle Music Conservatory, and we wanted to pay a personal visit to Mr. Gildersleeve. I left a voice mail, but I'm not sure he got it."

The man at the door narrowed his eyes. "Mr. Gildersleeve doesn't like unexpected guests."

"I understand. But this is an urgent matter."

"What urgent matter is that?" He cocked a thick eyebrow.

"It's for a totally amazing event we have coming up at the school," Jinky said.

"Don't you have alumni who do upcoming events at your establishment?"

This man was astute, I would give him that.

"We do," I answered. "We have some of the most talented alumni in the entire world. That is undoubtably true. But it seems a shame to have the talents of Felix Gildersleeve right here in Savannah and not try to use it somehow to teach our students how to be better musicians and to appreciate music more."

The man stared at us for another moment before turning up his nose. "Good speech, but I'm afraid Mr. Gildersleeve is very busy."

I nibbled on the inside of my mouth, feeling as if I needed a better plan than what I had. As soon as this man closed the door, I had no other means of getting in touch with Felix. No legal ones at least.

In the middle of my contemplation, a new sound distracted me.

A bird.

Inside the house.

A parrot? Like the one I'd heard in that voice mail?

I couldn't be sure. The sound was muted and far away.

But it was a possibility.

I *needed* to get inside that house.

"I think he did a wonderful job with the Star Wars themed orchestra he did last year," Jinky blurted. "I heard he's a big sci-fi fan. So am I. I'm absolutely obsessed!"

I hadn't expected that angle, but I waited to see how the man at the door would react.

He narrowed one eye. "You like . . . Star Wars?"

"I don't like it. I *love* it. My gut tells me Mr. Gildersleeve does also. Am I right? I could sense his passion in the project."

The man at the door only grunted.

We waited to see what he might do next.

Most likely, he would slam the door in our faces.

At least I could say I gave this a shot.

CHAPTER
THIRTY-TWO

"I'M SORRY, but it appears you've come all this way for nothing." The man raised his chin and gripped the door, ready to close it as he dismissed us.

Disappointment bit at me. I'd really thought we would be able to talk our way into seeing Felix Gildersleeve. But apparently that wasn't the case.

Still . . . that bird I heard inside . . .

I desperately wanted to see it. But short of barging in, I didn't see how that was going to happen.

We thanked him and turned to head back to Jinky's car.

That's when a new voice sounded behind us.

"What can I help you ladies with?"

Jinky and I both slowly turned around.

Felix Gildersleeve stood on the porch with a velvet bathrobe wrapped around him.

The man was probably only five-foot-five with dark hair that was thinning at the top, a rather pointed nose, and perceptive eyes—eyes that stared at me as if daring me to try to trick him.

Jinky and I exchanged a glance before I stepped toward him. Maybe we'd been given a second chance!

"I'm sorry to disturb you," I started. "I'm Camryn Paine, and I left a message for you, but—"

"What do you need?" His words were brisk as if he didn't have time to waste.

"We were hoping you could come talk to some of our students about the importance of choosing the right instrument," Jinky said.

He stared at us a moment as he processed her words. "Why do you want me to come? Certainly, there are other people you could talk to."

"But you're the expert," I said. "In fact, I even understand that you collect some of the world's most valuable and rarest instruments."

A smug expression captured his face. "That's true. But I don't usually speak at conservatories. I'm far too busy."

"I understand that," I continued. "But we just have so many students at the school who are big fans of yours. It would make their day to meet you."

His gaze darkened. "Usually, it would make their day to meet Beyoncé or Cardi B . . . or Camryn Paine. Not people like me."

Camryn Paine? So, he knew I used to be in the spotlight?

My cheeks heated for some reason—I wasn't even sure why.

I cleared my throat, determined not to be rattled. That could have been his motivation in mentioning my name.

"We have some of the most astute music students in the world coming to this conservatory." I tried to appeal to his sense of pride. "It would be such an honor if you would come and help make them even better musicians than they already are."

I held my breath as I waited for his response.

Gildersleeve stared at us a moment, his eyes flickering back and forth. Finally, he nodded. "Come in. Let's talk."

He turned and walked inside, waiting for us to follow.

Jinky and I quickly glanced at each other before hurrying after him.

His butler—I was going to think of him that way just for simplicity's sake—allowed us inside and closed the door behind us. He then escorted us through the foyer, past a grand spiraling staircase, and into a living room with a two-story-high ceiling.

Gildersleeve paused by one of the windows and stared into his backyard at the fountain bubbling in a grand courtyard. As he did, I heard the bird again.

Parrot?

I still wasn't sure.

"I don't like to be interrupted." He didn't bother to turn and look at us as he spoke. "I was working on my daily crossword when I heard the bell ring."

"I'm sorry, Mr. Gildersleeve," I started. "We really should have been more considerate. It's just that you're a hard man to get in touch with. Because you're so important."

Again, that seemed to appeal to his sense of self-importance, and he straightened.

"I *am* considered one of the leading experts in the world of musical instruments." He finally looked up at us, lifting his chin as he did.

"That's what we've heard." Jinky nodded, looking sincerely enthralled. "It's very impressive."

He stared at her a moment before shifting. "Would you like to see some of my collection?"

"We'd love to," I quickly said.

"Very well. Brevard, come with us. Please."

We followed behind Gildersleeve as he led us upstairs. Brevard the Butler followed behind us.

Part of me wondered if Brevard was coming with us to make sure that we didn't cause any trouble. Did this guy serve Gildersleeve tea and act as his personal security?

Gildersleeve stopped at the room at the end of the hallway and opened the door. When we stepped inside, I saw instruments displayed in glass cases all around the room, almost as if this place was a museum.

As we paced the perimeter of the room, Gildersleeve talked us through the importance of each instrument, details that would bore most people. Honestly, the fine details kind of bored me, but I didn't dare show that.

Instead, I listened and asked all the right questions.

The bird sounded louder in this room, but I still needed to get closer to it to know for sure if this was the parrot I'd heard on that voice mail.

"Do you like listening to Mozart?" Gildersleeve asked.

My gaze snapped toward him. "Mozart?"

Was this a trick question?

He grinned. "My bird. I can tell you're listening to him."

I ran a hand through my hair, hoping he couldn't read any more of my thoughts. "Birds make beautiful music, don't they?"

"That's precisely why I gave my macaw that name."

A macaw?

I held back my frown.

He was right. This was a different bird than the one I'd heard.

Disappointment bit into me.

That meant I needed to turn my attention back to these instruments.

"If you don't mind me asking, where do you even get these instruments? They're all such treasures."

Gildersleeve paused by a cello and gazed at it as if it were the most beautiful thing he'd ever seen. "At auctions mostly. Occasionally, I'll meet someone who's selling one. Other times, I'll come across an instrument I like and offer to buy it. It really just depends."

"To think of some of the people who played these instruments." I paused near him. "It's really awe-inspiring."

"I agree. It's good to talk to somebody else who appreciates that."

"Did you hear about that Stradivari violin that

was stolen?" I hoped my question wasn't too out of left field.

"I did. And that's a real shame. Why the Abernathys didn't have something of that value locked up is beyond me. Clearly, they didn't appreciate the instrument enough. If they had, they would have taken precautions."

The man did have a point.

"I agree that it's a shame," I said. "But who would've even stolen something like that?"

He sneered. "As I said, most ordinary people don't appreciate instruments like that. So, it doesn't make much sense to me either. If you ask me, those movers didn't care about that violin. I think it was all a setup."

"What do you mean a setup?" I held my breath as I waited for his answer. Could he be onto something?

Gildersleeve's gaze locked with mine. "I think someone else must have known that violin was there and asked those movers to steal it. That's the only thing that makes sense to me."

"Do you by chance know of anyone who has been looking for a Stradivari?" I tried to keep my voice light, but I knew my question probably sounded jarring.

He stared at me for a moment. "It almost sounds like you're investigating."

I laughed and shrugged casually—in my mind I did, at least. "I'm just curious as to the way these things work."

"The only person in this area that I know who would like to get his hands on that Stradivari actually works at your school." A sense of smugness seemed to saturate Gildersleeve's eyes.

My eyes widened. "Is that right? Who?"

"A man by the name of Lukas Amile."

I tried to hold back a gasp that the professor's name came up.

Had I been questioning a man who had actually been the guilty one all along?

It was something to think about.

———

"I found an employee of Bromtech who's willing to talk." Zeke's voice sounded into the cell phone an hour later.

"That's great news." My heart rate quickened. I'd been sitting at my desk at Grand Isle mentally reviewing my conversation with Gildersleeve. My thoughts quickly shifted, however.

"Do you want to come with me?"

Surprise washed through me. I quickly thought

through what I needed to do at the office and then realized all those tasks could wait. "I'd love to."

"Great. Where are you? I can pick you up."

I met Zeke at the front of the building ten minutes later and hopped into his rental car.

He was dressed in black dress slacks, a blue button-up shirt, and leather shoes. It was a nice look on him, especially with his dark hair. I was used to him having a more tactical look.

As I slipped on my seat belt, I wondered how much longer his SUV would be in the shop. But I didn't ask. I had too many other things on my mind.

"So, you found someone?" I started as we headed up the road to Charleston, which was two hours away.

His jaw tightened. "I did. I've been poking around, and I finally found someone who's willing to talk to me about what happened. But he's nervous. I'm afraid he's going to change his mind. That's why I want to get there right away."

"Who is this guy?"

"His name is Jay Stevens. He says he knows something that will help us."

I sat back in the seat with my thoughts racing. Could this be the break we needed? Would this Jay guy help us find the answers that we needed?

I could only hope. My life felt as if it had been

turned upside down this past week. I was ready to have more clarity.

For the rest of the ride, I told Zeke about my conversation with Gildersleeve and made generic small talk.

But the entire way, all I could think about was Phil and what his take would be on everything that had transpired.

CHAPTER
THIRTY-THREE

WE PULLED up to a coffeehouse located in a cute strip of shops.

Part of me felt guilty for missing work again—and for reasons that weren't related to the Abernathy case. Joseph didn't know the personal reasons I was gone right now. But I'd certainly put in enough overtime doing other projects.

I shouldn't feel guilty about being here now.

Still, part of me did.

Before we could park in front of the building, a man appeared at the passenger door and motioned for us to roll down the window.

I stared at him a moment, my heart pounding in double time.

The man was tall and thin with rather pointy features. His hair was almost black and styled in a classic clean-cut way that reminded me of my father —even though this guy was probably only in his late thirties.

"I'm Jay," the man called, sweat beading on his forehead despite the chilly air outside. "Can I get in?"

Zeke narrowed his eyes before nodding. "Get in the back."

I sensed Zeke was apprehensive about having a stranger in our car. For good reason.

What if this guy had a gun? What if this was some kind of con?

Having a father as a con artist really made me question everyone's motives. It was an unfortunate aftereffect that I often talked to my therapist about.

"Pull away." Jay's words came out quickly and high-pitched.

Zeke's neck muscles visibly tightened. "Are you in danger?"

"People are watching me." Jay scanned everything around us, his anxiety palpable. "I don't want them to see us together. I'm afraid of what that could mean."

Zeke eased away from the coffeehouse and pulled down the road. "Where should we go?"

The man looked back and forth as if he expected at any moment to have a vehicle appear and crash into us. His nervousness was making my anxiety skyrocket. My lungs felt tighter than they had before, and I also found myself glancing around.

"There's a parking lot at Walmart. Go there. There will be plenty of people around." He rattled off directions.

"Do you have any reason to believe that your life is in danger right at this very moment?" Zeke's voice hardened as he rephrased his earlier question.

Jay nodded, his entire body trembling—maybe even his gaze, if that were possible. "I've been on edge every day for the past three years. I know all it will take is one wrong move and that's going to end it all."

My pulse raced at his words. This guy was either in serious trouble or he was delusional. In different ways, I was rooting for both.

"Why did you agree to talk to us today?" Zeke asked.

"I can't keep living like this. It's not living at all. I'm so anxious that my wife left me. No one wants to be around someone like this. Including me."

I had no idea what this guy was about to tell us.

But a bad feeling gurgled in my gut.

And I couldn't wait to hear what he had to say. I hoped that he might provide some answers.

———

Zeke pulled into a spot between two empty cars but left the engine running after he put the vehicle in Park. Then he turned slightly toward Jay.

I saw in his gaze that he was remaining on guard.

That was probably a good idea. If this guy was telling the truth, danger could appear at any minute.

"Is something happening at Bromtech?" Zeke got right to the point.

"Yes." Jay nodded rapidly. "Definitely."

"Why don't we rewind this a little bit?" I started. "What do you do at the company?"

"I work in accounts payable."

"What kind of suspicious activities have you seen?" Zeke asked.

"Inflated invoices. Overcharging the government. False certifications that earned the company more per job than they deserve. I could go on."

I stored that information away. "Did you ever tell anyone what you saw?"

He wiped his brow with his shirtsleeve. "Just my supervisor. But he didn't seem to put much credence in what I told him. He said that was just the way the business works sometimes."

"How did you go from that suspicion to feeling like your life was on the line?" Zeke asked.

"I talked it over with another employee, Pam. She was angry when I showed her what I found. Really angry. She's not quiet like I am. She's a 'take the bull by the horns' kind of person, and she confronted Bromarski."

I had a feeling I knew where this was going—nowhere good.

"How did Bromarski handle that?" Zeke asked.

"Pam said he was very calm and acted like her claims weren't a big deal. He said the numbers needed to be double-checked, but it was probably a bookkeeping error. All in all, it seemed like a cordial meeting."

"But . . ." I prodded.

I knew there was a *but* in there.

"The next day when Pam and I came in, files were missing. I know it wasn't a coincidence. Then Pam suddenly left the company." Jay's jaw flexed, and he swallowed hard.

"On her own?" Zeke asked.

"That's what she said. When I talked to her on the phone, she seemed like a different person. It was disconcerting, to say the least." Jay swallowed hard. "But it didn't end there. I tried to call her a week later, and she was gone. Her apartment was empty. Her cell phone disconnected. And no one knew where she'd gone."

My heart pounded harder. "Did you ever find her?"

"No. I even called the police. They said they couldn't find any signs of foul play, and she probably just found another job. That was that. I figured if I ever said anything, I'd disappear too."

It certainly sounded like that could happen. "Why are you still with the company?"

He frowned and stared out the window a minute. "I want to quit, but I fear they'll think I'm a real threat then. In fact, I got a promotion to a job outside the department I specialized in. Now I don't have any access to any of the numbers. And I keep getting gifts and incentives for all my hard work."

"So, these guys are trying to buy you off?" Zeke clarified.

Jay nodded. "Mostly Bromarski. He's shady. But charming. Most people wouldn't suspect a thing."

Zeke glanced at me. "Maybe I need to talk to Bromarski again."

I shook my head as worry pulsed through me. "I'm not sure that's a good idea."

Especially not if this guy was as dangerous as it seemed.

THIRTY-FOUR

JUST AS JAY, Zeke, and I pulled away from the parking space, a black sedan with tinted windows appeared out of nowhere.

"Watch out!" Zeke yelled, jerking the wheel to the left.

The sedan barreled past us, nearly smashing the front of Zeke's rental.

It squealed away, nearly hitting another vehicle also.

We all sat there without speaking. My heart pounded out of control.

Someone had clearly been trying to send a message. That car's appearance wasn't a coincidence.

"Is everyone okay?" Zeke turned back to us.

"I'm fine," I muttered.

"Me too." Jay's voice sounded shaky and more

sweat had beaded on his forehead. "But that was on purpose. I know it was."

Neither Zeke nor I could disagree. Someone had followed us and tried to silence us before this conversation could go any further.

Next time, we probably wouldn't be having such a conversation.

Next time, these people wouldn't miss.

"It's not safe for you to go back to your house or work," Zeke muttered.

"Then what am I supposed to do?" Jay's voice climbed.

"I have someone who can help you disappear—for a while, at least."

"Disappear?" Jay's voice cracked. "But what about my life here?"

"You're divorced with no children, right?"

"That's right but . . ."

"Then your life here is on hold for now." Zeke continued to glance around as if waiting for the other driver to appear again.

Jay muttered something beneath his breath that I couldn't understand before saying, "I should have never met with you. This was a mistake."

"It's too late now. You can't undo it." Zeke's voice hardened as he took command of the situation. "You did meet with us, and now we need to figure out how to keep you safe. I'm going to get us out of here. Then I need to make some phone calls."

———

Three hours later, Jay was at an undisclosed location with one of Zeke's employees.

We'd done a brief internet search for Pam Davies. But it was just as Jay said—it was like she'd dropped off the face of the earth. Zeke said he was going to follow up with her family and friends to see if they knew anything.

Now, Zeke was driving me back to my apartment. We finally had a chance to talk, just the two of us. I couldn't wait to get his feedback on all that had happened.

"How deep do you think all this goes?" I asked Zeke.

His jaw twitched. "That's a good question. I wish Phil was here so I could ask him. I have a feeling he knew more than he was letting on."

I thought the same thing. "But if Phil knew something, why wouldn't he tell us? Maybe not me. But why wouldn't he tell you?"

Zeke shook his head, his expression still stony. "That's a good question. I don't know. Unless Phil had a reason to hide it. A good reason."

I crossed my arms and leaned into my seat. "I just can't imagine what that would be. Unless maybe it was the fact he was having an affair or an inappropriate relationship with someone who was involved in this."

My throat went dry as I said the words.

"Phil wasn't that type." Zeke's voice sounded calm and reassuring. "You know that."

I'd had a turbulent childhood. Then a turbulent relationship with Weston. So, when Phil came into my life, he was like a rock. He was everything I needed at that moment.

I really hoped I hadn't been this wrong about him.

I needed to know that something in my past had been real and not a figment of my imagination or a passing fancy. Phil had been that for me. A sign that people were good and trustworthy, and that true love was real.

I let out a sigh, determined to change the subject. "What do we even do next? Do you think Bromarski will meet you again?"

"I'm not sure yet. I need to drop you off at your place and then figure this out. I need to know you're safe."

"I could go with you . . ." I was hoping too much, wasn't I?

"I don't know what I'm getting into, Camryn. But I'd feel better if I went into this by myself. If I put you in danger . . ." He shook his head. "If something happened to you, I wouldn't ever forgive myself."

I nodded. I understood where he was coming from. I felt guilty over Weston's missing furniture.

"Whatever you do, be careful," I said instead.

Zeke looked over at me and nodded, and I felt that familiar attraction pass between us.

But just because we were attracted to each other didn't mean we needed to act on it.

He pulled up in front of my apartment and parked so he could walk me up. He checked everything out before turning toward me. "I'll be back. In the meantime, please be careful."

I nodded. "I will. I promise."

I'd been pacing in my apartment for the past two hours.

Yes, two hours.

Sometimes I liked sitting by myself and enjoying the quiet. But this wasn't one of those evenings. I had too much on my mind.

So, I still paced. Darkness had fallen outside. I was sure there were a million other things I should be doing. For starters, getting ready for The Christmas Thing. I had only two more nights until the big performance. I felt like I should be doing *something*.

Another part of me was tempted to call Weston and give him an update. But then I might have to explain more than I was willing.

That left me pacing.

I walked over to my window and glanced out.

What I saw outside made my lungs freeze.

A moving truck had parked on the street in front of my apartment building.

My gaze went to the front of it, and I saw the familiar dent in the passenger side door.

My breath caught.

That was the same truck that had been at Weston's place.

What was it doing out front now?

I stayed at the window, moving out of sight so anyone from the street wouldn't be able to see me. Then I watched.

No one appeared to be inside.

So where had the driver gone? Was he outside my door right now?

My skin crawled at the thought.

I should call the police, I decided. That would be the wise thing to do.

Quickly, I dialed Garrison's number and told him. He promised to come right away.

Just as I ended the call, a cry cut through the darkness.

My gaze shot to the other side of the street.

A man wearing a mask had grabbed a woman and was pulling her toward the moving truck. She kicked and screamed and tried to get away.

As her face came into view, I gasped.

Was that . . . Mariah?

My gaze focused.

It was.

My breath caught.

I couldn't just stand here.

Wasting no more time, I darted from my apartment.

I knew I'd promised Zeke I'd stay inside. But I couldn't watch someone snatch Mariah and not do anything about it.

At least, I could make a ruckus until the police got here.

And they should be here any minute.

I ran outside and paused on the sidewalk.

The noises had stopped.

I glanced to my left and right, looking for any sign of Mariah and the man trying to abduct her.

But I saw no one.

A new eeriness washed over me.

Why was it this quiet? What was going on here?

Then it hit me.

Something was wrong.

I stepped back, closer to the door of my apartment building.

As I did, arms encircled me, and a hand slapped over my mouth.

"You shouldn't have ever gotten involved in this," a voice grumbled in my ear.

A voice with a Boston accent.

CHAPTER
THIRTY-FIVE

BEFORE I REALIZED what was happening, arms lifted me. The next instant, the back of the truck opened, and I was shoved inside.

I didn't have time to pick myself up before the door slammed closed and a lock clicked in place on the other side.

Darkness surrounded me as the truck started.

Panic rushed through me.

What were these guys planning on doing with me?

A moment later, the truck moved.

They were taking me somewhere!

I couldn't just sit here and not do anything.

I rushed to my feet and began pounding on the sides of the truck, screaming for help. As I did, the driver accelerated.

My gut told me no one had heard me.

But Garrison should be here any moment.

Would he see the truck leaving and follow it?

I prayed that he would.

I continued banging on the side of the truck until my hands hurt and my voice became hoarse. Then I realized the best thing I could do right now was conserve my energy.

I slid down the wall onto the floor.

Well . . . the best thing I could do was conserve my energy and listen. If I paid close enough attention, maybe I'd hear something that would give me a clue as to what these guys were planning. Maybe I could figure out where they were taking me or how to get out of the situation.

I hoped that was the case.

We bumped along the road at a steady pace. We were going too slow to be on the highway and too fast to be in the city. I didn't hear any sirens around me. Occasionally, we stopped, which made me think we were at either a stop sign or traffic light.

But I heard little else.

I didn't hear other cars or horns or tires or music.

Which meant we were most likely leaving Savannah.

Despair tried to nip at me as I lowered my head into my arms.

I should have never gone outside. I'd known when I stepped out and everything was quiet that I shouldn't have left my apartment.

Speaking of which, where was Mariah? Had she been involved with trapping me? Or was she really in trouble?

I had no idea.

Even as the questions raced through my head, a chill washed over me. It was partly from fear and partly from the cold. The temperatures tonight were supposed to dip down into the mid-twenties. This truck was not climate-controlled, so I was starting to freeze in here. When I left my apartment, I had only been wearing some yoga pants and a long-sleeved shirt. I hadn't exactly been dressed for the weather.

At once, I reached for my pocket. I had tucked my phone there.

Disappointment filled me though.

It was gone.

I either dropped it or that guy may have taken it. But either way, calling somebody right now wasn't an option.

My only hope was that Garrison had arrived at my apartment and had put out a BOLO for this vehicle.

I tapped my head against the wall behind me,

wishing my skull wasn't so thick. I liked to pretend it wasn't. That I was easygoing.

But anyone who knew me well knew I was strong-willed.

That quality was the only explanation for why I'd gone outside tonight.

Just then, I heard voices coming from the cab of the truck.

I crawled across the floor to hear more.

"We're in over our heads," one man said.

"I know," the man with the Boston accent said. "I don't know what to do about it."

"We're many things, but we're not killers."

"We have to take care of this. We promised."

My heart beat harder.

These guys had been hired by someone.

But who?

And did that mean that someone else had killed Arnold . . . not his former colleagues?

———

I jerked my eyes open.

Darkness still surrounded me.

And cold. Bitter cold.

I pushed myself up, and I watched as my breath frosted in front of my face.

I'd fallen asleep, hadn't I? How could I have slept at a time like this?

But I had.

The last thing I remembered was leaning against the wall, counting down the time until something else happened.

But nothing had happened.

In fact, right now everything was quiet. I couldn't even hear the engine running. The tires weren't turning. There were no noises around me.

Had these guys parked the truck somewhere and left it?

I fought the surge of panic that wanted to claim me.

Panicking would get me nowhere.

Instead, I wrapped my arms over my chest and tried to warm myself.

Where would they have left me? In a driveway? In a storage facility? In the middle of nowhere? In an abandoned barn where no one would ever find me?

A cry of despair wanted to escape from deep within me.

I didn't let it.

I couldn't give up hope. Not yet.

On a whim, I rushed toward the doors and shoved them, hoping against hope that maybe they were unlocked.

They weren't.

I stood back, trying to figure out if there were any other ways to get out. But the moving truck's walls were metal. I had only my hands and feet to use as tools or weapons. There was no way I could break through. Even if I went to one of the seams and tried to kick it, I knew it would do no good.

But I couldn't just sit here and wait. Sitting here and waiting on the unknown seemed like the worst punishment possible.

I began pacing.

Had these guys left me here because I was getting too close to the truth? Were they planning on leaving me here to die?

I pressed my lips together as another cry wanted to escape. That would be a terrible way to go. Slow, miserable, and painful.

I squeezed my eyes shut.

Please, Lord . . . help me. Help someone find me.

I had no idea how much time had passed since I was abducted. It was still dark in here, and I didn't know how long I'd been sleeping.

I only hoped Garrison was out looking for me.

No doubt, Zeke probably knew about this by now and he was searching too.

Weston? I wasn't sure if anybody would have

been in touch with him or not. But it seemed likely he'd been contacted just in case he knew anything.

I kept pacing to keep myself warm.

But how long would I have to do this until I gave up?

I HAD PACED around this truck for 10,124 steps. Yes, I'd counted.

I didn't know how that translated into time. Right now, it really didn't matter.

Finally, I sat down in the corner and pulled my arms across my chest, trying to stop myself from shivering so bad.

I decided to focus on what I was going to do once someone found me.

Should I keep looking for this violin? Was the violin worth more than my life?

I knew the answer to that.

It was a resounding *no*.

Yet another part of me felt stubbornly determined. If someone thought I was going to give up just because they threatened me . . . they were wrong.

Except I really had to weigh what I was doing with the possibilities for my future.

Plus, there was more going on here than just the violin.

I remembered my conversation with Jay Stevens. Phil must have discovered something somehow. All of that tied in with Andrea also. There are so many unanswered questions.

Who was Pam? What had happened to her?

Was Bromarski greedy enough that he'd had her killed and covered up her death?

As I closed my eyes and let my head fall back against the moving truck wall, images of the kiss Zeke and I had shared filled my mind.

The kiss itself was nice. And Zeke was nice.

If the circumstances were different . . . could the two of us have a future?

I wasn't sure. I wasn't even sure he was my type.

Then there was Weston. We had such a long history between us. And a person never really forgot their first love.

As thoughts about the two men volleyed back and forth in my mind, a noise sounded in the distance.

My breath caught.

Were those tires on gravel?

That's what it sounded like to me.

I rose to my feet.

Had these guys returned?

And if so, just what were they planning?

Fear rippled through me at the possibilities.

I continued to brace myself, unsure what to expect.

If these were the same people who'd abducted me, I knew there was most likely two of them. I knew I wouldn't be able to fight them both off, especially not since I felt so weak. All the adrenaline in the world wouldn't help me now.

Despite that, I fisted my hands in front of me as I prepared myself for whatever would happen next.

I wasn't going to make this easy on them. I wouldn't be doing them any favors.

The car tires stopped. Doors opened and slammed. Footsteps started my way.

I could hardly breathe as I waited to see who would open that door—or even if they were going to open that door. For all I knew, these people could drive this moving truck somewhere else.

Something rattled. Probably the lock on the door.

My breathing became heavier, shallower, as I waited. Anticipated. Dreaded.

Then the door cracked.

Sunlight filled my vision, the glare blinding.

Three blurry figures stood on the other side. I had to blink against the bright light as I tried to make out faces. Voices.

"Camryn?" A familiar voice cut through the air.

"Zeke?"

After I blinked several more times, Zeke, Weston, and Garrison came into view.

I nearly collapsed with relief.

Instead, I took a shaky step forward.

I stared back and forth between Weston and Zeke.

Who should I go to first?

Before I could decide, Weston rushed toward me and wrapped his arms around my waist. "Camryn, are you okay?"

I nearly collapsed against him. "I am now."

I wasn't going to die alone.

A cry escaped my throat at the thought.

Thank God, I had people looking out for me . . .

THIRTY-SEVEN

"HOW DID you guys ever find me?" I sat in the police station with a warm cup of coffee in my hand as well as a glazed grocery store doughnut. Someone had put a blanket over me, and I was sufficiently starting to thaw out.

Garrison and one of his officers sat at the conference room table in front of me, and Zeke and Weston flanked either side. Clearly, both men had been worried. Maybe even Garrison too.

"We put a BOLO out on the truck." Garrison's expression looked stony, like he was irked beyond measure with everything that had happened—and maybe with me also. "Thankfully, you'd called me so I knew you'd seen that vehicle outside. That helped. I didn't think we were going to get any hits—but then, this morning, we did. Someone reported seeing the vehicle sitting out in that field. We had no idea what to expect when we got there."

"So . . . someone randomly called it in?" I clarified, wondering if I was super fortunate or if one of the movers got a conscience and couldn't go through with his plan to leave me there to die.

Garrison nodded. "That's right. This woman didn't even leave a name or phone number—just the tip. Thank goodness, she did."

"I'm glad you guys arrived when you did." I took another sip of the strong, thick coffee, feeling like I'd never be able to drink enough to get warm. But my chill went much deeper than the mere physical.

I'd come face-to-face with the possibility that I could die. That wasn't something someone walked away from unchanged.

"What were you thinking going outside by yourself?" Zeke stared at me, his gaze probing—and maybe accusing. I couldn't blame him.

My mind raced back in time to what had happened.

"Mariah." I suddenly straightened. "Someone tried to grab her."

"Mariah?" Garrison stared at me, waiting for an explanation.

"Arnold Myer's ex-girlfriend. She was outside my

apartment, and a man grabbed her. That's why I went outside. I had to help."

Garrison jotted something down before turning to an officer. "Go check on her. See when the last time someone saw her was."

"I should have mentioned her first—" What had I been thinking? Panic raced through me at my oversight. It should have been my number one priority.

"Your thoughts are frazzled." Weston's hand came down on my shoulder. "That's understandable."

But I wasn't so sure about that.

Then I remembered the conversation I'd overheard the men in the front seat having. There was so much I needed to share, and I was failing big time.

"There's one more thing—I think someone hired these guys." I shared what I'd overheard.

"Do you have any idea whom they may have been talking about?" Garrison stared at me as he waited for my response.

I shook my head as disappointment bit deep. "I have no idea."

Weston dropped me off at my place—Zeke had agreed only because he wanted to get out there and investigate. Plus, the police promised to station an officer outside my building. Thankfully, Garrison had found my phone on the sidewalk out front. He'd given it back to me, and it still worked.

I'd invited Weston in, but he was going to stop by to see his kids before they left for Christmas break. Their mom was pulling them out of school so they could spend the holidays in Saint-Tropez. I'd insisted to Weston that he should go and that I would be fine.

I took a shower, the warm water washing away memories—not all of them, but the steady spray did help. I changed into clean clothes and fixed myself a sandwich.

Then I sat at my kitchen table and wondered what to do with myself now. It seemed anticlimactic to simply sit here after everything that had happened.

But what were my other options?

I stared at the Christmas tree Zeke had helped me decorate and remembered our kiss.

That was the last thing I wanted to think about.

I stared out the window and remembered the moving truck that had been parked there before I'd been abducted. That made me think about the moving scheme Weston and I had set up, had made me remember standing in front of his house holding hands and calling each other pet names.

That was also the last thing I wanted to think about.

I sighed.

When my phone rang, I hoped that things might turn around. I was right.

"I'm trying to reach Camryn Paine," an unfamiliar voice said on the other line.

"I'm Camryn."

"Camryn, my name is Wendy. I need to talk to you."

Caution crept up my spine. "What is this pertaining to?"

Occasionally, I got media calls for the school, and other times I got calls from reporters wanting to do "Where are they today?" features on former celebrities.

"It's about Andrea," Wendy rushed. "I was her best friend, and I heard that you were asking around about her."

My breath caught. "How did you know that?"

"I asked her landlady to let me know if anyone ever came around. She mentioned that you called her a couple of weeks ago."

My breath caught. This woman was legitimate.

How many people knew I'd called the landlord? Only Zeke as far as I knew.

But I hadn't shared my name . . .

I nibbled on my lip at that realization.

Perhaps this woman had done a simple internet search for the number and my name had appeared.

It was possible. My number was included with press releases.

"What do you want to talk about?" I asked.

"Not on the phone. I'll only talk face to face."

"I can meet you." As my thoughts raced forward, I glanced at the time. "Are you available now?"

"I can meet in an hour. But I need you to come alone."

My racing heartbeat slowed to a worried adagio. "I'm not sure that's a good idea."

"I'm not going to talk unless you do." Her voice sounded panicked but firm.

"Where do you want to meet?" I wasn't even sure I should be asking that question, but I didn't want this opportunity to slip away either. However, given the ordeal I'd just been through, I needed to be cautious.

"There's a coffeehouse located in Beaufort," Wendy said. "We could meet there. Make sure that you're alone."

Was this woman paranoid? Or did she have a reason to be concerned?

When I remembered Jay, I knew I had to take this

seriously. There was a good chance this woman could be in real danger.

"I mean it," Wendy finished. "If I see you with someone else, I'll leave. This isn't a trap. But I can't risk anyone else knowing we're meeting. I have a family. I have to look out for them."

Based on the tone of her voice, I felt as if she was telling the truth. Wendy honestly sounded frightened. If she did have a family, then it made sense why she was taking these precautions. I'd do the same.

But I needed to think about myself also. I couldn't put myself in another dangerous situation. How could I navigate this situation to ensure that?

After another moment of hesitation, I promised to meet her.

But as I lowered my phone and thought things through, I didn't know exactly how I should handle this.

THIRTY-EIGHT

FIFTEEN MINUTES LATER, Skittles was driving down the road with me in her passenger seat. It wasn't exactly like I could go on my own since I didn't drive or have a car here with me.

Still, I didn't want to pull Skittles into something she shouldn't be a part of. But I had few other choices right now. Zeke was researching something else, and Weston was teaching. I'd almost asked Jinky, but she also had a class coming up.

So right now, it was just me and Skittles. My assistant was rambling on and on about her K-dramas and K-pop groups that she liked to listen to. In fact, she and three of her friends were one of the acts performing at The Christmas Thing. I'd heard them rehearsing, and they sounded great.

Finally, Skittles parallel parked two spaces down from the coffeehouse.

As she put the car in Park, I turned to her, ready to break some news she probably wouldn't like. "Thank you for driving me here, but you can't go inside with me."

"For real?" Her head fell to the side.

I nodded with a frown. "I'm sorry."

"But is it a good idea for you to go by yourself? Safety in numbers, right? Never go alone unless you have a phone. By yourself could leave you dead on a shelf."

I couldn't even begin to comprehend the nonsense she was spouting right now. "I probably shouldn't go alone, but I don't have any other choices right now. I just ask that you stay here and watch for any signs of trouble. If you see anything suspicious happen, call Garrison and Zeke."

"Not Weston?" She stared at me, carefully watching my reaction.

I scowled at her. "Garrison and Zeke have law-enforcement experience and Weston does not."

"I get that." She stared at me another moment before letting out a sigh. "But I'm kind of worried about you."

"I should be fine. Just be my wingman right now."

"Your wingman?" That seemed to perk her up, and she grinned. "I like the sound of that. I've always wanted to be a wingman."

"Skittles . . ." I wasn't sure what she was thinking, but whatever it was, I needed to nip it in the bud.

Skittles raised her hands. "I'll be good. I promise. Now go before you're late."

———

I sat at a table in the corner of the coffeehouse with a vanilla latte in front of me. Every time the door opened, my gaze latched onto the person who entered.

So far, Wendy hadn't shown up. At least, no one had shown up that I assumed was Wendy.

Was this meeting just a waste of my time?

I sighed and glanced at my watch. The woman was fifteen minutes late. I'd give her five more minutes, and then I was leaving. I had entirely too many other things to do than just sit here on this wild goose chase.

Five minutes later, just as I grabbed my purse and stood, the door opened, and a woman there caught my gaze.

She walked straight toward me, a concerned expression on her face.

The woman was in her thirties, with long, straight wheat-colored hair. Her features looked pinched, and her heart-shaped face looked downcast.

"I'm sorry I'm late. But I had to make sure your friend wasn't coming inside." She sat down across from me.

I lowered myself back into my seat, my spine stiffer than it had been earlier. "I don't drive, so I had to have someone bring me."

She looked at me, questions in her eyes that she didn't ask. "I'm sorry that we had to meet like this. But I couldn't think of any other way."

"What's going on, Wendy? You definitely have me curious."

She swallowed hard, her gaze almost looking hollow. "I've been sitting on some information for a long time, too afraid to tell anybody. But now it's time to share."

I wanted to ask her what had changed, but that didn't seem important right now.

"I'm here," I told her. "I'm very curious."

"Andrea and I go way back, all the way to elementary school." She licked her lips before she continued. "She used to work for Bromtech."

I blinked, certain I hadn't heard her correctly. "She did? But . . . I researched her. Certainly, I would have noticed that fact and made that connection."

"When she left the company, she changed her name. She didn't want anyone to find her."

"Why not?" That story sounded awfully familiar.

"She discovered some sketchy accounting practices, and she threatened to go to the feds about them. When the CEO of the company found out, he threatened her. Not in an obvious way. It was subtle, but she knew what he meant."

"So, she moved and changed her name?" I tried to let the pieces fall into place.

"She knew she'd die if she didn't. So, she told everyone she had a new job and she left. But she died anyway a couple of weeks later."

I sucked in a breath. "Wait . . . was Andrea . . . Pam?"

Wendy nodded. "She changed her name so she could be safe. I'm the only one who knew."

I held my breath as I waited for her to continue.

"She met your husband while he was doing security for Bromarski, and she said she felt like he was someone she could trust. She confided in him about what was going on."

My heart pounded in my ears. "Go on."

Was I really ready to hear the rest?

I had no choice at this point. I had to know.

"He was trying to help her," Wendy said. "He was one of the people who helped her secure her new identity, actually. He also thought she should go forward to the feds anyway. She was considering it. But then she died."

I rubbed my throat which now burned. So, Phil had simply been helping Andrea out? They weren't having an affair?

Relief filled me, but it was short-lived. There was still a lot to be concerned about.

"It sounds like Bromarski is dangerous, someone not to be messed with," I said, keeping my voice low as a new group of people entered the coffeehouse.

Wendy leaned closer. "According to Andrea, he's mixed up in all kinds of things, things that could send him to jail for a very long time."

"Why are you telling me this now?"

"Because I don't sleep at night thinking about what this guy has gotten away with. And then I heard that your husband died. I knew that it wasn't a coincidence."

"Three years have passed . . ."

"I know. It shouldn't have taken me this long. But . . . I don't know what to say. It did. When her landlord called and said she had a visitor, I decided to do some research. I found out your name was connected with the phone number. Then I did research on you and discovered who you really were and . . ."

I stared at her a moment and nodded. "I appreciate you coming forward now. Is there something you want me to do with this information?"

Her gaze locked with mine. "I don't want to see this guy get away with what he's done. I was hoping you might do something to help. I'm not brave like you are."

"Brave like I am?" I almost wanted to laugh.

"I did research. I saw that you solved that murder at the college. I thought that maybe you could solve this too. But you can't mention my name. I don't want any part of that."

This woman was truly terrified. And, after all I'd seen, I couldn't blame her. "I understand."

Wendy glanced around. "I need to go. Before someone sees me here with you."

"You think you're being followed?" I glanced around but didn't see anyone suspicious.

"I don't know for sure. But Andrea didn't think she was being followed either. And look what happened to her."

CHAPTER
THIRTY-NINE

AS I LEFT THE COFFEEHOUSE, I glanced around me, looking for any signs that somebody was indeed watching.

I still didn't see anyone—only a cheerful sidewalk decorated with evergreen and red bows.

But I couldn't shake the feeling that maybe someone was watching.

Tension pulled across my chest.

I hoped I hadn't put Skittles in a dangerous situation. I also hoped Wendy got home safely. If we were able to proceed with this any further and make a case against Bromtech, we might need her as a witness.

I spotted Skittles up ahead and quickened my steps. A moment later, I hopped in the passenger seat and told her to go.

Her eyes lit. "This is so exciting. I feel like I'm in a spy thriller or something."

Only in spy thrillers, the hero always survived. In real life, they didn't.

I would remind her of that fact if it came down to it.

An image of Phil filled my thoughts, and I frowned. But this wasn't the time to let grief get the best of me. This was a time to survive.

But what if Phil had died because he'd been trying to do the right thing and bring down someone greedy and dishonest?

I choked back a cry at the thought.

As Skittles pulled back onto the main street cutting through town, I glanced behind us. Another vehicle about eight car lengths away pulled out also.

Coincidence? I couldn't be sure. But we needed to play it safe.

"Turn left here," I told her.

Some of her excitement seemed to wane as the smile slipped from her lips. "You're serious?"

"Dead."

Her expression went still. "I don't like the sound of that."

"You shouldn't." I usually liked to nurture and comfort people. But this wasn't the time. Skittles needed to understand the potential seriousness of this situation.

As she took a left, I glanced behind me again.

A moment later, the dark car followed.

The tension in my chest only tugged harder and tighter.

I could *not* let anything happen to Skittles. I should have never asked her to come.

Now I just needed to get her out of this alive.

"What now?" Skittles' knuckles were white on the steering wheel.

"Go right." I pointed to emphasize my words.

"Righty tighty, lefty loosy . . ." she muttered.

"That's only when you're tightening or opening a jar," I reminded her. "Doesn't apply right now."

She had the habit of getting her safety advice mixed up when she got stressed.

One more turn and, if the other vehicle still followed, I'd know it wasn't a coincidence.

My heart pounded in my ears as I waited to see what would happen.

Sure enough, the other car turned also.

I swallowed hard.

Should I call someone? What good would that do? No one would be able to reach us in time.

If Skittles and I were going to get out of this situation, it was up to me.

That thought terrified me.

Think, Camryn. Think.

What would Phil do in this situation?

He'd work with what he had.

I glanced ahead and spotted a traffic light that had just turned yellow. Maybe this was our chance.

"See if you can make it through the light safely."

"Okay . . . hold on." Skittles pressed her foot against the accelerator.

I wanted to close my eyes. I didn't want to see.

But that wasn't an option.

We barreled toward the intersection. Just as it turned red, we squeaked through.

I looked behind me and saw that the cross traffic had already started.

It looked like we'd bought ourselves a few minutes.

"Turn here!" I pointed to a new street.

"Here?"

"Just trust me," I told her. Although Skittles had no reason to trust me.

This was the first time I had ever done anything like this. It was like asking a first-year medical student to do a life-saving surgery on you.

I shoved that thought aside.

Skittles turned. At the first alley in between buildings, I directed her to turn again.

She did as I asked and then pulled behind a dumpster near the end.

Then we waited.

"Are you sure this is a good idea?" Skittles looked at me with wide, fear-filled eyes. "I thought when you were in these situations you should keep moving. Moving means you're grooving, but being still can be a deadly chill."

Was she right? I couldn't remember.

But, right now, moving wasn't an option.

I'd made my choice, and now I had to hope I didn't regret it.

CHAPTER
FORTY

I KEPT WATCHING BEHIND ME. A few minutes later, I saw the black car zoom past.

The keywords being *zoom past. Not stopping.*

But I knew Skittles and I weren't in the clear yet. That driver could still turn around. He could still find us.

And we couldn't just be sitting here waiting if he did.

"Come on." I opened the door.

"You want to get out?" Skittles' eyes widened with alarm. "That seems like a bad idea."

"We can't just stay here. We need to be proactive right now—just in case."

Skittles turned the car off and grabbed her purse. A moment later, we scrambled behind the building and through a back door leading into a Mexican restaurant.

The tantalizing scent of sizzling peppers and onions hit us as we hurried through the kitchen, ignoring the odd looks from the restaurant staff and cooks preparing the food. Once in the dining area we wandered through the crowds inside, heading to the picture windows out front.

I was nearly certain, based on the angle we'd parked, that the other driver wouldn't spot Skittles' car. But I wanted to see for myself.

As I went to the window, I told Skittles to put our name in at the hostess stand. I told her to mention that we were waiting for people and couldn't be seated yet. That might explain why I was looking out the window right now.

A few minutes later, the black car went past again, even more slowly this time.

But it didn't turn down the alley.

I released the breath I'd been holding.

I continued to watch just out of sight as the vehicle turned right going the opposite way. It was too soon to feel relieved. But I was almost convinced we'd lost them.

Skittles and I would stay in here for ten or fifteen more minutes. Maybe even pick up some food to go. I wasn't sure.

The only thing I *was* sure about was that I wanted to get back to Savannah ASAP.

———

Skittles and I got back to Grand Isle two hours later. During the ride, I'd called Wendy. She was okay.

I told her about our experience and encouraged her to take her family somewhere for the evening to lie low. She'd cried a little but had agreed.

Our narrow escape was all Skittles wanted to talk about for the remainder of the ride home. Now that we were safe, she was nearly hyper with excitement.

I wished I could revel in this as if it were a real-life action movie. But instead, I kept watching around us, expecting trouble to appear at any time.

But it hadn't happened. Thank goodness.

As soon as we arrived at the school, I remembered that dress rehearsal was tonight. I rushed to Hannon Auditorium to help get everything ready.

Weston met me at the entrance, almost like he'd been waiting for me. "Everything okay?"

I nodded as I brushed a piece of lint from my skirt. I really didn't want to get into what had just happened. There would be too many questions. Too much scrutiny.

"I'm fine," I said instead. "Just a little frazzled I suppose."

"You should have seen her in action."

Skittles suddenly appeared behind me. Where had she even come from? I thought she was grabbing something from my office.

"We were being followed, and Camryn knew exactly what to do," Skittles continued, her eyes dancing with excitement.

Weston's gaze latched onto mine. "You were followed?"

"Don't worry," Skittles answered for me. "Thanks to Camryn's expert thinking, we managed to evade capture so we could be ready for the rapture." She moved her hands in a "raise the roof" motion.

"Capture?" Weston didn't break his gaze.

I raised my hands—but mine were in surrender. "Skittles is exaggerating a bit. No one tried to capture us. We were followed. But now everything's fine and we're here."

My voice sounded much lighter than I felt.

"That's good, I guess." But based on Weston's narrowed gaze, he was still leery.

Before we could continue talking, Beck Tarsus strode into the auditorium and headed for us. "Hey, did you two think any more about doing that duet together?"

My mind drew a blank at his words.

I hadn't given his request any real thought over the past couple of days. I'd been too distracted with the attempts on my life, I suppose.

But I couldn't put it off any longer.

"Unfortunately, I don't think it's going to work out," I told him. "I'm sorry."

As he frowned, several more students appeared to listen to our conversation.

"Are you sure?" Beck asked. "I really think it would be a showstopper."

I noticed Weston was watching me also. He was all in favor of singing together again, wasn't he? I just wasn't sure I was ready for it.

"I'm afraid at this point it's impossible." I shrugged apologetically, ready to end this conversation but hating the fact that I was disappointing the students around me.

"Man . . . it was going to be epic," one of the students muttered with a head shake.

"I already told my mom, and she said she was going to invite her friends," someone else said.

"Mine too!" someone else added.

I exchanged a look with Weston.

I didn't know so many people were counting on this.

I didn't know so many people were still so aware of my music, for that matter.

But there was little I could do about my decision now. I'd given my answer . . . and I had too much work to do to worry about whether it was right or wrong.

CHAPTER
FORTY-ONE

ZEKE SHOWED up at the auditorium right as our dress rehearsal ended.

And it had been a fabulous rehearsal. Our show was going to be *fantastic*. I had no doubts about that.

No one would even miss Weston and I performing.

Zeke joined me as I headed backstage to straighten up.

"Anything new?" I beat him to the punch.

"As a matter of fact, there is." His tone was dead serious. "Maybe you should sit down."

My breath caught. That didn't sound good.

I nodded, feeling a little shaky as I glanced around. "Let's go out there." I nodded toward the seats in the audience.

We quietly walked side by side, my thoughts racing.

He'd discovered something, hadn't he?

Would this news change my perspective of my marriage?

I hoped that wasn't the case.

I lowered myself into a chair at the back of the auditorium. He sat beside me.

Everyone else lingered in the stage area, giving us some privacy.

"I met with one of my friends from the FBI today and told him what was going on," Zeke started. "He thinks that there's enough evidence for an arrest warrant for Bromarski."

"What?" Surprise coursed through me. "Really?"

That almost seemed too easy.

"We convinced Jay to turn some files over," Zeke continued. "He's still in protective custody until this blows over. But we're making some serious progress right now."

"That's great news."

He nodded, but his gaze didn't look any lighter. "It is. This isn't over yet. But this is a step in the right direction."

A burst of joy rushed through me, and I started to reach forward to hug him. But I stopped myself. That was probably a bad idea considering our earlier kiss. I didn't want to give off any wrong vibes.

Instead, I cleared my throat and asked, "What now?"

"There's still the question of whether or not it was one of Bromarski's guys who's been trying to harm you or if it was the person who stole that violin."

"Or it could be a mix of both." I shrugged.

Clearly, there were some things that were the fault of the men who'd stolen the violin—such as the incident last night where I had been left in the moving truck.

But getting shot at? Somehow that didn't seem to fit these guys' MO.

Was it possible that all along I had two different sets of people trying to harm me?

The thought wasn't comforting. But it was a real possibility.

Zeke rose. "If you're done here, I should get you home. Maybe this will all be over soon."

As he said that, Weston strode through the back doors, a box of programs in hand. His steps slowed when he saw us.

"You heading home?" he asked.

"Do you need help?"

"I can handle things here."

"Are you sure?" I asked, hating to leave him alone.

"I'm positive."

I stared at him another moment, giving him a chance to change his mind. But that didn't seem like it was going to happen.

Finally, I nodded. "Okay then. I'll see you tomorrow."

Weston seemed to force a smile. "Tomorrow."

———

My thoughts wouldn't stop racing on the ride home.

I felt like I was missing something.

But what?

Who could the bad guy be?

Who would have hired those guys to steal the violin? Honestly, it could be anyone—anyone with means. All it would take was a few phone calls and a few transfers of money.

In order to find out who the thief was, we almost had to capture his henchmen first.

I didn't think Felix Gildersleeve was behind this. Or Mariah. Or Carl.

Professor Amile still intrigued me, however.

"What are you thinking about?" Zeke asked as he stared at the dark road ahead.

"You feel like taking a detour?"

"If it means you're not going to go somewhere alone, then yes."

I pulled out my phone and quickly looked up an address on the conservatory's directory. Then I rattled off directions to Zeke, and he turned down the road until we reached a small bungalow about ten minutes from campus.

"Where are we?" Zeke asked as we sat parked in front of the house.

"This is Professor Amile's home." I nodded to the house in the distance.

"And why are we here?" He still looked confused.

"Because his name keeps coming up in my investigation. Because he keeps offering his help, even though it's very unlike him. Because . . . I'm out of options." I shrugged, deciding to be real instead of pretending like I had my thoughts together.

Before Zeke could respond, someone stepped from Amile's front door.

It was none other than Professor Amile himself.

And he had a violin case in his hands.

My breath caught.

"Could that be . . . ?" I murmured, my gaze fastened on him.

"Certainly, he's too smart to step outside with a stolen violin," Zeke said. "He'd be more secretive."

I would like to think that also. But I also didn't believe in coincidences. "We need to follow him."

"Really?" Zeke glanced at me.

"Yes, really. I need answers, Zeke. I need for all of this to be done."

"Okay then." He shifted the car back into Drive.

Like an expert, Zeke stayed a comfortable distance behind Amile as he tailed him through the streets of downtown Savannah.

Finally, Amile pulled to a stop in front of a pawn shop.

I glanced at the time. It was only 8:30.

Most likely, the place would close around nine.

"What now?" Zeke glanced at me, waiting for my decision.

"I need to find out why he's going inside." I reached for the door handle.

"Do I need to remind you of everything you've already been through?"

I couldn't forget, even if I wanted to. "I'll be safe. I have you with me."

He stared at me another moment and then nodded. "Okay then. Let's go."

We climbed out. I needed to get inside that pawn shop without Amile seeing me. But the place looked small.

How likely was it that I could slip inside without being spotted?

It didn't seem likely.

But maybe Zeke could go inside, and I could remain in his shadow. Amile shouldn't recognize Zeke. He was broad enough that he could conceal me.

"You go first," I muttered to Zeke.

"As you wish." He slipped inside and began perusing some instruments along the wall. As he did, I was careful to remain concealed.

But, really, I was listening to every word Amile said.

"I'd like to sell this violin," he said.

"Let's take a look," the clerk said.

It sounded like something was set atop the glass counter. Then I heard the clerk say, "Oh my. This one is valuable. You sure you want to sell a beauty like this?"

Zeke and I exchanged a glance.

It couldn't be this easy, could it?

Because it sounded like Amile was trying to pawn the Stradivari.

CHAPTER
FORTY-TWO

I COULDN'T REMAIN where I was anymore. I had to confront Amile.

I slipped around Zeke and rushed toward the counter. A sense of justice flared to life inside me as I realized Amile was the culprit this whole time.

"What do you think you're doing?" I rushed.

Amile's eyes widened when he spotted me. "Mrs. Paine . . . what are you doing here?"

"The bigger question is: what are you doing here?" I stared at him, not willing to give him any breaks.

Amile glanced at Zeke, who stepped behind me. Then he nodded toward the violin. "I'm selling this."

I glanced at the violin. I might have an extraordinary ear, but I definitely didn't have an eye for violins. Mostly, they all looked the same.

"The Abernathys' violin . . . ?" I stared at him, watching his expression.

He stared at me a moment before letting out a laugh. "The Stradivari? You've got to be kidding me. If I had that violin, there's no way I'd bring it here. There's no way I would try to pawn it right now when everyone is looking for it. I'm smarter than that."

I frowned, not liking his tone. "Then what is this?"

His smile disappeared. "It's one of my violins, obviously."

"Why are you pawning it?"

"For the money, of course. I could use some extra cash at Christmas."

I heard the catch in his voice. He wasn't telling the truth.

I couldn't let that slide.

I narrowed my gaze as I stepped closer to him. "Why are you really trying to sell it?"

He scowled before letting out a long, laborious sigh. "That's right. You're like a human lie detector or something, aren't you?"

My hands went to my hips. "You're avoiding my question."

Amile let out another long breath and stared in

the distance as if contemplating his options. "I'm in some debt if you must know."

"What kind of debt?" Zeke asked, his voice deep and loud.

Amile scowled again. "Not that it's any of your business, but sometimes I like to cut loose. To gamble. To play some slots online. Nothing that's a big deal."

I paused, waiting for him to continue.

He frowned. "Until it was."

I stared at him another moment, trying to figure out if I believed him.

I did.

Guilt and shame filled his gaze, and his shoulders slumped.

This prideful man had a weak spot—like most people. He'd just kept it hidden.

"And now you have to sell your instruments in order to pay back the loans you took out?" I didn't want to, but I actually felt sorry for the man.

"It's the consequences of my fallibility, I suppose."

"How much money do you need?" I asked.

He broke eye contact as if ashamed. "Five thousand dollars."

"I'll give you four thousand for this violin," the pawn shop guy said.

Amile lowered his head.

He was telling the truth. I felt certain of it.

So, if I could rule him out, then whom did that leave?

———

As we stepped toward Zeke's car, I heard a footstep behind us.

Instantly, my back muscles tightened.

Zeke must have heard it also because he gripped my arm.

"Come on," he urged.

But before we reached the car, a shot rang through the air.

He jerked me down to the ground behind a mailbox.

"Stay here!"

He grabbed his gun, ready to fire.

Before he could, I heard another footstep behind me.

The next instant, someone grabbed me.

I swallowed a scream.

Zeke lunged toward the masked man gripping my arms. "Let her go!"

"Put that gun down!" the man ordered as he pressed something into my side.

A gun, I realized.

My throat went dry.

This man had a gun pressed into my ribs.

Zeke paused before nodding. "Okay. Just don't hurt her."

He placed his gun on the ground and rose, hands in the air.

As he did, another man approached from the other side.

I could hardly breathe.

What were these guys planning? Had I escaped death more than once only to be confronted by it again?

Where were other pedestrians when we needed them? The street suddenly seemed empty. Had anyone called the cops?

"You're going to do what we say," the man behind me muttered. "Or else."

CHAPTER
FORTY-THREE

THE ONE THING I knew for sure was that I couldn't go with this man.

I'd end up dead if I did.

Just like Andrea.

And Phil.

I swallowed another cry.

These guys had just been waiting for the right moment to catch us alone, hadn't they?

"Let her go," Zeke growled. "She has nothing to do with this."

"Then you two shouldn't have nosed into our business," the man behind me snarled. "Now, let's move."

My gaze met Zeke's.

He thought that was a bad idea also.

Before I could second-guess myself, I rammed my elbow into my captor's abdomen.

He let out a gasp.

The distraction was just enough for Zeke to sucker punch the man beside him.

As the man bent over, I tried to reach for his gun.

But it flew from his hand and just out of reach.

I hoped I hadn't made a bad move—one that ended up getting one or both of us killed.

There was no going back now.

The man near me quickly gathered himself and turned back toward me with a sneer that was visible in the dark and with his mask on. He lunged toward me, but I ducked.

He rammed the mailbox but quickly righted himself and grabbed my arm.

I thrashed, desperate to get away.

I couldn't let him win.

Especially if these were the guys who'd killed Phil.

As sirens sounded in the distance, the two men froze.

Looked at each other.

Then at us.

"This isn't over," one of them muttered.

Then they took off running in the opposite direction.

Zeke quickly turned to me. "Camryn . . . are you okay?"

I nodded as I tried to catch my breath and control my raging pulse. "I'm fine."

"Stay here and wait for the police," he ordered.

Then he took off after the men.

———

"So these guys just came after you out of nowhere?" Garrison stared at me and Zeke as we stood on the sidewalk after being shot at.

Zeke had chased those men, but like any savvy criminal, they'd had a getaway car waiting. There was now a BOLO out for the vehicle, and I hoped the Savannah police might track them down.

We'd filled Garrison in on the situation with Bromtech.

"I suspect these guys have been following us," Zeke said.

"Did you get a look at them?" Garrison said.

"They were wearing masks." Zeke's jaw tightened as if he were disappointed. "It was hard to tell anything about them."

I stepped closer. "There is one way you might be able to ID them . . ."

Both men turned to me.

"What's that?" Garrison asked.

I held up something in my hands. "When that man grabbed me, I pulled this out of his pocket."

Their eyes widened when I showed them the wallet.

"What?" Zeke nearly sounded breathless. "You managed to pick his pocket?"

"Honestly, my father was able to teach me a few tricks of his trade," I admitted. "In the craziness of struggling against him, I decided to make sure he didn't get away with this."

"That's impressive." Garrison pulled on some gloves and took the wallet from me. "Good work."

I actually felt myself beaming with pride for a moment. "Thank you."

He opened it and flipped through the contents of the wallet. "We have a name. Dan Lancaster. Sound familiar?"

I shook my head. "I have no doubt these guys are hired hands."

"I agree," Zeke said.

Garrison slipped the wallet into a bag and then grabbed his phone. "Good work tonight. I'm going to call in some backup to help track these guys down. In the meantime, you two stay safe."

Maybe—just maybe—that ID would provide some answers we desperately needed.

FORTY-FOUR

I WOKE up the next morning, and Zeke took me to the police station before I needed to head to Grand Isle.

Though it was within walking distance, I knew I'd get in trouble if I ventured out alone. That's why I let Zeke drive me.

I wasn't surprised when we stepped inside and saw Garrison working on a Saturday. That was the nature of his job—and probably the reason he looked so tired all the time.

I could relate.

"What brings you by?" Garrison turned off his computer screen as he shifted toward us.

"I wondered if there were any updates?" I started.

"As a matter of fact, yes. We found the two men

who shot at you last night, and the FBI brought Bromarski in for questioning."

"That's great news!" The update was unexpected—but wonderful. "What about Tommy? Mariah?"

Garrison's eyes brightened. "I'm glad you asked. Tommy is doing better. We haven't been able to talk to him yet, but the doctors said he's looking good. And Mariah was found up in Hilton Head last night. She claimed someone paid her to disappear for a few days."

My heart rate quickened. "Was she a part of this? Did she know who these guys were?"

"She said she'd never seen them before and that she felt as if she didn't listen to them, they'd kill her."

"Could she describe these guys?" Zeke asked.

Certainly, she'd been able to tell the police *something*, right?

"They were wearing masks." Garrison frowned as if he were disappointed also.

I *knew* that was going to be the answer, but I'd hoped for something different.

"We're still working on the case, but we just haven't gotten very far yet," Garrison continued. "Even though we have an image of the men inside the stolen truck, no one has IDed them. The violin hasn't turned up anywhere, and there haven't been any ransom calls. We're pretty much batting zero."

"I'm sorry to hear that," I muttered. "What about the FBI? Have they made progress?"

He twisted his head as if confused. "What do you mean? With Bromtech?"

"Have they made any progress?" I repeated, unsure where the breakdown was.

Garrison stared at me a moment as if I'd lost my mind before shaking his head. "They're not working this case. Why would they?"

"But . . ."

Garrison raised his eyebrows. "But what?"

"But I heard the Art Crime Team had stepped in."

"Who did you hear *that* from?"

I tried to remember. Was it Skittles? Or Mrs. Abernathy? Either way, the feds' involvement had sounded like a sure thing.

"I'm sorry, Camryn. There's nothing else I can tell you. We are taking this seriously, especially with Arnold Myers' murder and your abduction. But the trail has gone cold."

I took a step back and nodded, hating that there weren't any more updates and that my thoughts felt so scrambled. "Thank you for your time."

"Of course," Garrison added.

His phone rang, and he put it to his ear. He stood as he mumbled several things to the caller. As he put his phone away, he turned toward Zeke and me.

"We just got a tip on one of the men involved with the moving scheme. It seems credible—and the tip came from that press release you sent out with the grainy images of the suspects."

My heart lifted. "That's good news."

"Let's hope. I'm heading out to check out this man now."

"I hope you get your guy," I told him.

He let out an exhausted sigh. "Me too."

As I left, I had a new spring in my step.

Bromarski had been arrested, and I prayed justice would be done in that situation.

Despite that good news, I hadn't found Mrs. Abernathy's violin yet.

I frowned but tried not to let that fact dim my sense of victory.

Today was the day.

The Christmas Thing.

I couldn't wait to see how the production went.

But I wouldn't be able to enjoy Christmas break if I didn't have any resolution to this other case.

AS SOON AS I stepped outside the police station, Zeke turned toward me. "Why do you look so shocked?"

"I *know* someone told me the FBI was involved." I paused on the sidewalk and shook my head. I wasn't going crazy. But I did have a lot on my mind lately. Stress could play with a person's thoughts sometimes.

"Maybe whoever told you was mistaken. Or maybe you're thinking about the fact that I told you I'd talked to someone at the FBI about Bromtech."

He had a point, but . . . "It's bothering me."

"It doesn't really matter if the FBI is involved or not, you still don't have any answers."

I frowned as I paced closer to his car. "I know.

And, honestly, I'm not sure how much longer I can keep looking for the violin."

He gave me a look. "It's not like you to quit."

"I don't want to quit. But I don't want to keep chasing something I'm never going to find either. I don't like wasting my time." Wasn't that the life lesson that kept coming back to me? Chasing things that evaporated at your touch was never a winning choice, whether that was a career in music, finding your identity in a title, or trying to turn back the hands of time.

"I understand." He opened my door for me so I could climb inside. "I'm sure you'll make a wise choice."

But would I? I didn't feel like the wisest person in the world lately. I'd made too many mistakes.

However, I would be asking someone about the FBI. I wanted to find out where I'd gotten my wires crossed.

———

Zeke dropped me off at Grand Isle and left to talk to his FBI contact.

As I'd walked into the building, Weston called, and I gave him the update. We also talked about some last-minute details for today.

All in all, things were going well.

I hoped they stayed that way.

I walked into my office several minutes later and spotted Skittles working on some filing.

Perfect. She was just the person I wanted to talk to.

I dropped my purse near my desk and turned toward her. "Skittles, are you the one who told me the FBI was involved in the Abernathys' case?"

She thought about it a moment and shrugged. "Maybe. I heard that somewhere."

"From whom?"

"Mrs. Abernathy, I think."

I leaned back against the table behind my desk, still chewing on that. "Did Mrs. Abernathy tell you that because she talked to the FBI? Or did someone else tell her the FBI was getting involved?"

Skittles shrugged again, pausing with some manilla folders in her hands. "I have no idea. I'm sorry. I wish I could help."

"Maybe you can." I hadn't been able to stop thinking about what was going on.

I was missing something.

But what? Could Skittles be the sounding board I needed to make sense of this case?

"What do you need?" Skittles turned toward me, looking ready and willing to help.

I sat down in my seat, suddenly tired yet lively at the same time. "Do you remember that voice mail we heard on Arnold's phone when his body was found?"

"I do. Why?"

"I heard a parrot in the background, which is a great clue. But . . . throughout all this, I haven't heard any parrots to indicate someone as a suspect." Especially since Gildersleeve had a macaw. I'd felt so excited for a brief moment—until I realized it was the wrong bird.

A wrinkle formed between her eyes as a skeptical expression claimed her features. "Sorry if this is too honest, but finding a parrot seems like a long shot. Nearly impossible, really."

"I know. But hear me out. What if someone who knows the Abernathys arranged for this violin to be stolen? Someone could have hired these guys and made it look like they stumbled upon the violin by chance when in fact it was a setup from the start."

"I'm still not sure where you're going with this. Do you have a suspect in mind?" She shifted her weight and looped her fingers through the suspenders attached to her oversized black pants.

I licked my lips before diving in. "I'm going to take a stab in the dark here. But do you know of anyone associated with the Abernathys who owns a parrot?"

Skittles thought about it a minute before shrugging. "I wish I could help, but I can't say I do."

"Do you know anyone at all who owns a parrot?" I was really reaching here, wasn't I? But if I could connect the parrot with the Abernathys then maybe I stood a chance of finding answers. Because the more I thought about it, the more certain I felt that this violin theft had been premeditated. It was the only thing that made sense.

"Not really." She squinted. "You're a little obsessed with this parrot, aren't you?"

"It's a great clue. It just hasn't led anywhere."

Skittles suddenly froze.

"What?" She had a thought, didn't she?

She quickly shook her head as if doubting herself. "This is probably nothing."

"Let me be the judge of that."

Her gaze locked with mine, but she still didn't say anything. Questions danced in her eyes instead. Finally, after a moment of silence, she blurted, "There's a parrot at Mr. Abernathy's office."

I swallowed hard. "Is that right? What does he do for a living again?"

"He owns a real estate company called Verve."

"What do they do, exactly?"

Skittle shrugged. "They acquire, develop, and manage properties. The whole shebang." Her eyes widened. "Wait . . . do you think . . ."

"Someone at his company should know all about moving and what it entails . . . in fact, maybe someone at his office knew about the violin. Maybe someone there is behind it."

"Mr. Abernathy did talk about the violin sometimes," Skittles said with a frown. "Usually in an almost mocking manner."

He resented that violin, didn't he? Had Mrs. Abernathy's music career taken her away from him? Had he secretly encouraged her to walk away from that path?

"Tell me more about Mr Abernathy."

She shrugged. "He's nice enough. He didn't come from money like his wife did. He built his business on his own."

"Has he been acting normal lately? Has Tara said anything?"

Skittles' face seemed to grow paler.

"What is it, Skittles?" She knew something. I was certain of it.

"Tara actually said her father has been acting a little strange lately, like he had something on his mind."

Maybe it wasn't an employee at Verve who arranged to steal the violin. What if it was Mr. Abernathy? What if he had a secret motivation and had set all of this up?

Skittles stared at me a moment. "You think Mr. Abernathy could be guilty?"

I shrugged. "It seems like he could be a good suspect. There's the parrot, to start with—"

"But if we're just talking about the parrot as a clue then anyone at the company could really be guilty."

"True. But we also have to look for means, motive, and opportunity. Mr. Abernathy had the motivation—he wants that violin gone. He's got the money to pay someone to do his dirty work—that's the means. And as far as opportunity . . . he's the one who set up the move."

"But murder?"

She was right. Murder didn't seem to fit this scenario.

Unless that murder had been accidental.

"Money can make people do strange things," I finally muttered.

"That's an interesting theory, but how can you prove it?"

That was a great question.

"I could call someone I know who works for

Verve," Skittles said. "She's the office gossip. Maybe she knows something."

"You sure you're comfortable doing this?"

She nodded. "I'm sure."

I hesitated just a second before saying, "Then let's do it."

I STOOD AT SKITTLES' side as she called Tammy, one of her former coworkers at Ivan Abernathy's business.

We were taking a chance by doing this, but I hoped it paid off.

We needed a little more information—and this seemed like the best way to get it.

Tammy answered on the first ring. "Tammy—it's Professor Skittles."

"Professor!" Her voice lilted with excitement. "It's great to hear from you. What's going on?"

Tammy said everything as if she were a DJ at a night club trying to get the crowd wound up. It was quite entertaining, and this conversation had just started.

"Hey, I'm trying to figure out a present for Ivan,"

Skittles continued. "It meant a lot to me that he offered me the job there last summer, so I want to get him something. But I'm not sure what. You have any ideas?"

"Oh . . . that's a nice gesture," Tammy continued. "Skittles is in the house!"

Okay, now I was almost rolling my eyes. But I didn't.

Instead, I continued to listen, still hoping our plan would work.

"Do you know of anything he likes or has mentioned lately?" Skittles asked.

"That's a good question . . . let me think. Hmm . . ."

We waited.

"I know!" Tammy finally said. "I'm not supposed to know this, but I was talking to Jeannine, his secretary, and she mentioned something."

I straightened. Could it be this easy?

I wasn't sure.

"What is it?" Skittles asked.

"He has a secret addiction to . . ."

Gambling?

Drugs?

Women?

". . . Hot Cheetos."

Skittles and I looked at each other. Hot Cheetos? Really?

"That's . . . great." Skittles frowned as if the answer frazzled her. "But I was hoping to buy something a little more substantial. I'm actually hoping to get another internship there this summer. I think it would look great on my résumé."

"Really? I figured you'd do something with music."

Skittles frowned. "I want to do both, but there's no money in music. I figure I need to save up some now while I can."

"True fact, am I right?" She paused. "Okay, so something fancier . . . wait. I might know something."

"What's that?"

"I heard something kind of crazy, and I'm not sure if it's true or not." She lowered her voice to a whisper. "But rumor has it that Mr. Abernathy is trying to buy an island."

Skittles and I looked at each other again.

"An island?" Skittles repeated.

"That's right. Isn't that crazy? I heard it's in the Caribbean."

"Is this an investment?"

"No, apparently, it's personal. It's always been a dream of his, and he finally has enough money to do it. I heard he's going to surprise his family at Christmas, so don't mention it to anyone yet. I don't want to get fired over this. But, if he actually does that, maybe you could get him something island-themed."

"That's a great idea. I'll have to keep my ears open for that. If it's true, then I have just the gift. A mosquito net."

Tammy let out a loud chuckle. "I'm not sure about that. I was thinking more along the lines of a tiki torch. But you do you, you know?"

They chatted a couple more minutes before Skittles ended the call.

Skittles glanced at me, guilt in her gaze. "You really think Mr. Abernathy could be behind this?"

She clearly had a personal connection to this family, which would make this difficult. She was in a tough spot since Tara was her best friend. I was sure that when she'd asked me to help, she'd never anticipated this to be the outcome.

"Selling that violin would give him a lot of money," I said. "Enough to give him some capital to buy that island."

She frowned. "That is true."

"Plus, he could have arranged all of it over the phone while keeping the perfect alibi. He was out of town for the move itself, right?"

"I think that's what Tara said. Now that you

mention it, I guess I'm kind of surprised the Aber-nathys didn't use movers recommended by Mr. Abernathy's company."

She had a good point. "That makes this even more suspicious."

Skittles sighed, and her shoulders slumped. "Unfortunately, I think you're right. What if he is guilty? And, if he is, did he also kill that man?"

Her question hung in the air.

———

Two hours later, I was still mulling over my theory about Ivan Abernathy.

Skittles and I had agreed to think about it for a while longer rather than throwing out accusations. But I thought we could be onto something.

I'd been down at Hannon Auditorium working on The Christmas Thing but had to run back to my office to grab my notes for tonight's performance. Just as I snatched the clipboard from a table behind my desk, a shadow filled my door.

My hand rushed over my heart, which now beat overtime as I glanced up and saw who was standing there.

"Mrs. Abernathy," I muttered. "I wasn't expecting you."

She shrugged as if she had all the time in the world—and therefore I should also. She was dressed casually today—casual as in red high heels and a form-fitting black dress that showed her every curve—even the less-than-flattering ones.

"I know you're busy," she began. "I just wondered if you had any updates? I haven't heard from you in a couple of days."

I paused beside my desk, clipboard in hand, as my thoughts about her husband rushed through my mind. "I wish I did. But I'm sorry. Right now, my attention is on this production."

"I figured as much." She scowled. "It's just that . . . every day, that violin could be farther and farther away."

"I understand your frustration. And I'm sorry. I've been doing what I can . . ."

"I know you have, dear." She almost sounded like she was placating me.

I stared at her another moment, more questions pooling in my mind. Should I ask her anything that might confirm my theory that her husband could be behind this? Or was I setting myself up for trouble if I did that?

I wasn't sure.

Either way, I needed to broach the subject very, very carefully.

I leaned my hip against my desk. "Mrs. Abernathy . . . I had another thought about the investigation, and I've started to wonder if maybe this was an inside job. Is there anyone you know personally who might have wanted to take that violin?"

"Someone I know?" She opened her mouth as if aghast. "No one I know would do this."

"Are you sure?"

She narrowed her eyes and her voice lost some of its friendly tone. "Are you accusing one of my friends?"

I shrugged, trying to remain casual. "Or maybe a family member . . ."

"A family member? How dare you!" Mrs. Abernathy clutched her purse and glowered at me.

I raised my hands in surrender. "It was just a theory . . ."

My words didn't seem to appease her that much because her eyes remained narrowed. "Why in the world would you think that?"

And this was where it got a little tricky . . . "Because of the parrot at your husband's office."

"You think *my husband* did this?" The outrage in her voice only grew shriller.

I decided to play my hand carefully. I crossed behind my desk and sat there. Slipping my phone from my pocket, I held it beneath the desk. I texted

Zeke to come to the office—just in case things turned ugly.

I hoped I'd hit all the right buttons because I was sending this text blindly.

My thoughts raced as I stared at Mrs. Abernathy.

Had I been wrong?

What if Ivan Abernathy wasn't behind this?

Maybe there was another person who made more sense.

I LICKED my lips as I gathered my courage. "You want to know what I think?"

A discerning expression remained on Mrs. Abernathy's face as she stood blocking the doorway. "I'll certainly hear you out. But if you think I'm going to let you talk poorly about my family, then you have another thing coming for you."

And here I went . . . "I think someone you know discovered this moving scam. Instead of turning in the people involved, he or she asked them for a favor."

"What kind of favor?" Skepticism dripped from her words.

"To steal that violin."

"Why in the world would someone I know want someone to steal that violin?"

"Maybe it's a family member who knows that the instrument has brought nothing but heartache to everyone in your family," I suggested. "What better way to end the curse without hurting any feelings."

"I can't deny the fact that it's brought heartache." Mrs. Abernathy raised her eyebrows, looking as pious as ever. "But if what you're saying is true, then someone in my family would also be responsible for murder. Is that what you're implying?"

I prayed Zeke had gotten my message as I gripped my phone beneath the desk. "Not necessarily. But I *am* thinking that Arnold Myers realized just how valuable the violin was. Maybe he tried to turn the tables on the person who hired him. And maybe this person lashed out not meaning to kill him. But, in anger, our suspect hit Arnold over the head . . . and by then it was too late."

"You got all of that from a parrot?" She stared at me as if I'd lost my mind.

I shrugged. "Maybe."

"It's an interesting theory, but it's not true. It can't possibly be. No one in my family would do this."

"But what if my theory is true?" I studied her face —and listened to her voice—very carefully. "And what if after you hired me, this person got nervous because I was getting too close to answers? That's when he or she hired those same con artists to abduct me. Maybe even to hurt me. But those guys couldn't do it—because they're not murderers. They're only thieves."

Mrs. Abernathy let out a scoffing laugh. "You certainly have spun a yarn. But I'm afraid this all has just been a game to you. Maybe I shouldn't have hired you."

I wasn't going to give in to her mind game. I had to stay strong.

"Why did you say the FBI was involved when they weren't?" I leaned back in my chair, still watching and listening.

Something flickered in her gaze. "It was my understanding that they were. Why do you ask?"

"Because they were never going to be involved. I'm not sure where you got that information."

"My husband didn't tell me that, if that's what you're implying." Mrs. Abernathy turned up her nose as she lowered her eyelids.

"Actually, it's not. I'm not pointing the finger at your husband at all."

"Then what are you doing?"

My gaze locked with hers. "I'm saying I think you're guilty."

"What? I would never—"

"But you did." I rose to my feet and tucked my phone into my pocket. "You just never meant to take it this far. But then you got in over your head. You and Arnold got into a fight, didn't you? And you didn't mean to kill him. But he made you so mad when he tried to double-cross you that you swung your purse and hit him over the head. Next thing you knew, he was dead."

She said nothing, only shot daggers at me with her gaze.

"And when I started getting closer to answers, then you really got nervous. You hired a different crew to help with the move. Then you got your other hired hands to abduct me."

"You're ridiculous."

"But am I? I think you probably hired them to kill me also, but those guys aren't killers. They wanted out. So they left me out there in the middle of nowhere, waited several hours, then reported a suspicious moving truck to law enforcement."

She continued to scowl. "You have quite the imagination. I'll give you that."

I stepped closer, knowing I needed to go all in if I was going to make this work. "I'm going to bring you down. You know that, don't you?"

"If you think I'm going to let some ex-pop star bring me down, you're sorely mistaken."

I paused in front of her. "You couldn't let your daughter use that violin, could you? It was cursed."

"It was going to ruin her life!"

I sucked in a breath. Was that a confession? Or something close enough?

I thought it might be.

"Everyone who touches it suffers," Mrs. Abernathy continued. "I just wanted to get rid of it and keep my family name. It wasn't supposed to turn into all of this!"

"So you hired those men? You set all of this into motion?"

"I should have just done it myself. It never pays to have other people do your dirty work!" Mrs. Abernathy lunged toward me.

But before she could reach me, someone grabbed her arm.

Detective Garrison.

I'd heard his distinct footsteps coming three minutes ago. Yes, I could even distinguish footsteps sometimes. Garrison's were light and fast, and he often walked on his heels.

Knowing he was coming was the only reason I'd goaded Mrs. Abernathy.

"Mrs. Barbara Abernathy, you're under arrest for the murder of Arnold Myers." Garrison placed handcuffs on her.

Zeke and an officer lingered behind him.

"What? You have nothing to hold me on! You're out of your mind." Outrage laced her voice.

"For the record, I think you hired me and told the FBI you didn't want their help because you didn't think I would find the violin," I continued. "You knew the FBI had a better chance, and you couldn't risk that."

"Detective, you can't take her seriously!" Mrs. Abernathy turned back to Garrison.

"I am both arresting you and taking her seriously," Garrison said. "Besides, we found the two men you hired. They just confessed to their role and confirmed everything Mrs. Paine said. The game is over."

"What?" Mrs. Abernathy's face suddenly fell.

Garrison nodded. "It's true."

"You've got to believe me! I didn't mean for any of this to happen. I just didn't want my daughter taking on the curse. She was determined to play that violin in Detroit. I couldn't let her ruin her life. You'd do the same thing in my shoes!"

"Mrs. Paine, I'm going to need a statement from you later." Garrison glanced back at me.

"Can it wait until after The Christmas Thing?"

"Absolutely."

———

As Garrison and his officer led Mrs. Abernathy away, Zeke stepped into my office.

"Good work." His hands rested casually in his pockets.

I sat down at my desk and leaned back in my chair. "Thanks. I wasn't sure how that would play out for a minute. But as soon as I heard Garrison approaching my office, I knew I could take the chance."

"Just to let you know, Bromarski has officially been charged with corruption. Three guys that he hired to act as his henchmen have also been arrested."

"Did Bromarski admit to killing Phil?" I held my breath as I waited for his answer.

Zeke shook his head, compassion filling his gaze. "Not yet. But I think we can safely assume he was responsible for Phil's death and Andrea's—or Pam's, to use her real name."

I wasn't sure if I should feel better or worse. Most likely, a mix of the two.

It would take me a while to sort through all those emotions.

"I can't believe the lengths some people will go through for money and power," I finally murmured.

"It can consume them."

A lot like music. I kept that thought to myself.

"I thought I'd let you know that now that I'm no longer needed here, I'm going to head back to Atlanta soon."

My heart leapt into my throat. "Already?"

He pressed his lips together as if hesitant to say whatever he needed to say. "Carlena called this morning. We're talking about trying to work things out between us. I thought I didn't want to be tied down. The truth is, I don't want to be hurt again. After my divorce I've been holding back. But I can't let fear dictate my future."

"I think that's wise. I'm really happy for you." I meant the words. Even though I liked Zeke, the fact that he'd been Phil's best friend made the possibility of any future relationship too strange for me.

"You sure? Even after . . ." He shrugged as if he didn't want to say the word "kiss" aloud.

I waved my hand in the air. "It was just a moment, that's all."

He stared at me another minute and nodded. "I know you're going to find someone else one day. Maybe you already have."

My cheeks heated. Was he talking about Weston? I didn't dare ask.

"We'll see," I muttered.

He nodded behind him. "By the way, would you

be offended if I didn't stay for The Christmas Thing?"

"Are you kidding? I'll be offended if you do stay."

He let out a chuckle. "Good to know."

I rose and gave him a quick hug. "You take care of yourself."

"You too."

"And tell Carlena I said hello."

FORTY-EIGHT

AFTER CHANGING into a black sequined gown, I practically had to run to get back to Hannon Auditorium before the show.

By the time I arrived, it was only fifteen minutes until showtime. The good news was that I could now fully enjoy the entire production.

I couldn't wait to see these students shine tonight.

This was going to be a real win, not only for the school, but for the community, and I was proud to have helped put The Christmas Thing together.

As I stepped backstage and ran over a few last-minute details with my stage manager, someone called my name.

I looked over and saw . . . Scarlett standing there.

I nearly dropped my clipboard. "Scarlett!"

"Mom!"

We rushed toward each other and embraced. As we did, I inhaled the fragrance of her sweet strawberry-scented shampoo. My mind was swept back in time to when she was a little girl. It seemed like just yesterday.

"What are you doing here?" I asked when Scarlett pulled away.

"I had to come see you for Christmas, of course." Her skin practically glowed as she faced me, a grin stretched across her face.

"No cruise with your boyfriend?"

She gave me a *no duh* look. "You didn't really think I was going to do that, did you?"

I shrugged. "Maybe . . ."

"I'd never do that to you." She squeezed my arm. "Christmas is about family. You taught me that."

Tears welled in my eyes when I realized I wasn't going to have to spend the holidays alone after all. "I'm so glad you're here!"

"I'm so glad to be here."

We hugged again.

"Camryn, we've got to get started," the student director said behind me.

"I'll talk to you more afterward, okay?" Scarlett said. "For now, I have a seat out in the audience."

I nodded, realizing only just then that tears had welled in my eyes. "Okay. I look forward to it."

An hour into the show, I was still glowing from seeing Scarlett.

Being with my daughter made me so unbelievably happy and at peace.

And the show . . . everything so far had gone smashingly.

The acts. The videos. The energy from the audience.

Only thirty more minutes, and this would be a wrap.

And I could feel good about my cases, my husband's faithfulness, and The Christmas Thing.

I couldn't ask for a better happy ending.

Beck Tarsus was onstage singing, "All I Want for Christmas Is You." His voice and stage presence captivated the audience. I could really see a bright future for him, and I was excited that he was getting his start here.

"Good job, Camryn," someone quietly said beside me.

I turned and saw Weston standing there in his black tux and white cowboy hat. He looked like a million bucks.

He'd been helping back in the sound booth, trying to iron out some technical problems for most of the day. He would pop backstage for long enough for the two of us to emcee before disappearing again.

It appeared all his technical issues had finally been worked out.

I grinned as I looked up at him. "You too. Things couldn't have gone better this evening."

"I agree." He shifted closer to be heard over the music.

As he did, I caught a whiff of his leathery scent.

Something about it made my heart beat a little faster.

"By the way, I saw Scarlett," he continued. "I know you're thrilled to have her here."

My grin widened. "Beyond thrilled."

"She's your spitting image, you know."

"She's much prettier than I ever was."

"I don't know about that." Weston twisted his head. "You were the prettiest woman I'd ever seen before. You still are."

My cheeks flushed at his words. "Thank you."

His gaze was warm on mine as he turned to face me more fully.

"I mean it." His voice almost sounded hoarse with emotion.

I cleared my throat, trying not to let my feelings get the best of me. Because I had the strange desire to reach up and touch his cheek. To rekindle what had been lost.

What I really needed to do was change the subject. Only a couple of days ago, I'd experienced my first kiss since Phil's death, and it hadn't gone well. I wasn't sure if it was because it was Zeke or because I just wasn't ready to take that next step.

"Did you decide what you're doing for Christmas?" I asked, figuring the subject was safe enough.

His expression dimmed, and he glanced at the stage. "I'm going to head to Nashville and take Mark up on that offer to tour with him."

Part of me wasn't surprised. Maybe it would be good for Weston, all things considered. "I think that sounds fun, like it will be a nice distraction."

"I hope so. Christmas will certainly be different this year."

I remembered Scarlett was in town, and I counted my blessings. But, still, it would be different. Holidays were always the hardest after you've lost someone.

"Yes, it will be," I whispered. "But, if anything changes, you're always welcome to come to my place."

Weston's gaze caught mine again. "I appreciate that."

As we stared at each other another moment, I

wondered what he needed to tell me. He'd started to say something last week, but we'd been interrupted. It had seemed important.

I opened my mouth and almost asked.

Then I shut it again.

Maybe it was better if I didn't know.

If I didn't know *yet* at least.

As familiar notes began playing on the stage, I froze, all my earlier peaceful thoughts gone like the Beatles after their final performance.

I glanced at Beck and saw him grinning at me as he strummed his guitar.

"Is he . . . ?" My brain tried to piece together exactly what was happening.

"Beck and his band are playing our song." Weston smiled as the band played the opening to "Me and You."

"Oh, no . . ." I stepped back, panic racing through me.

"The song doesn't bring back memories that are that bad, does it?" Weston caught my arm.

"It's just that . . ." What was I trying to say? I rubbed my burning throat.

"Just what?" Weston waited, not at all frazzled or hurried by the song playing on stage.

My gaze met his. "There's so much history with that song." My words nearly came out as a whisper.

"That's not a bad thing." Weston nodded toward the stage. "What do you say we give it a shot?"

Was he talking about the song?

Or us?

As the audience cheered, I swallowed hard.

Everyone seemed to be counting on us.

Rooting for us.

What could it hurt to sing together just this once?

I glanced at Weston and nodded, trying to push away my reluctance. I remembered what I'd been thinking about earlier. About how short life was. About how death had taught me lessons I hadn't wanted to learn.

But I didn't want that lesson to only be confined to investigations. Maybe I needed to apply it to singing also. At least this one time.

"Okay." My voice trembled slightly. "Let's do it."

The stage manager handed us mics, and Weston took my hand as we walked out on stage together.

The audience cheered like crazy when they saw us.

I had no idea people liked our song so much.

Or that they'd liked Weston and me together.

We turned to face each other.

As the music changed, I knew it was my cue to begin singing.

I prayed I wouldn't make a fool of myself as I started.

The lyrics left my lips, sweeping me back to old times.

Magic seemed to pass between Weston and me as our voices blended together, as our gazes caught, as my heart seemed to instantly bond with the man in front of me.

Was I exaggerating?

I didn't know.

I only knew that I'd never ever felt as connected with someone as I did when I sang with Weston.

As we sang the last note and ended the song standing face-to-face, the audience rose to their feet in a standing ovation.

Weston and I grinned at each other.

"We've still got it," he murmured.

I nodded. "Yes, I think we do."

~~~

Thank you so much for reading *Crime Strikes a Chord*. If you enjoyed this book, please consider leaving a review.

Stayed tuned for *Tone Death*, coming Summer 2022!
~~~

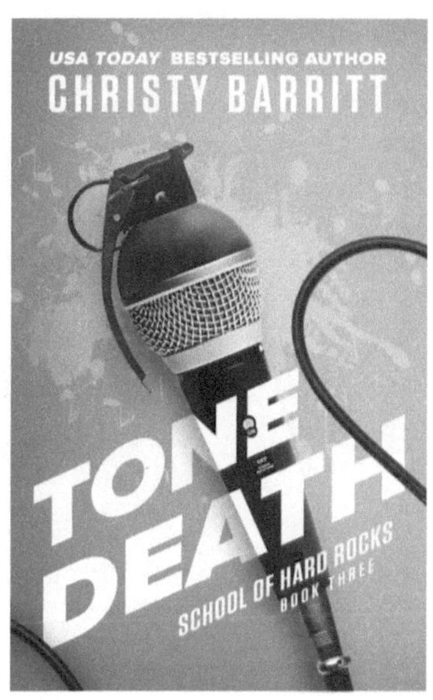
USA TODAY BESTSELLING AUTHOR
CHRISTY BARRITT
TONE
DEATH
SCHOOL OF HARD ROCKS
BOOK THREE

ALSO BY CHRISTY BARRITT:

YOU MIGHT ALSO ENJOY

∎∎∎

THE SQUEAKY CLEAN MYSTERY
SERIES

On her way to completing a degree in forensic science, Gabby St. Claire drops out of school and starts her own crime-scene cleaning business. When a routine cleaning job uncovers a murder weapon the police overlooked, she realizes that the wrong person is in jail. She also realizes that crime scene cleaning might be the perfect career for utilizing her investigative skills.

#1 Hazardous Duty

#2 Suspicious Minds

#2.5 It Came Upon a Midnight Crime (novella)

#3 Organized Grime

#4 Dirty Deeds

#5 The Scum of All Fears

#6 To Love, Honor and Perish

THE WORST DETECTIVE EVER:

I'm not really a private detective. I just play one on TV.

Joey Darling, better known to the world as Raven Remington, detective extraordinaire, is trying to separate herself from her invincible alter ego. She played the spunky character for five years on the hit TV show *Relentless*, which catapulted her to fame and into the role of Hollywood's sweetheart. When her marriage falls apart, her finances dwindle to nothing, and her father disappears, Joey finds herself on the Outer Banks of North Carolina, trying to piece together her life away from the limelight. But as people continually mistake her for the character she played on TV, she's tasked with solving real life crimes . . . even though she's terrible at it.

#1 Ready to Fumble

#2 Reign of Error

#3 Safety in Blunders

#4 Join the Flub

#5 Blooper Freak

#6 Flaw Abiding Citizen

#7 Gaffe Out Loud

#8 Joke and Dagger

#9 Wreck the Halls

#10 Glitch and Famous

ABOUT THE AUTHOR

USA Today has called Christy Barritt's books "scary, funny, passionate, and quirky."

Christy writes both mystery and romantic suspense novels that are clean with underlying messages of faith. Her books have won the Daphne du Maurier Award for Excellence in Suspense and Mystery, have been twice nominated for the Romantic Times Reviewers' Choice Award, and have finaled for both a Carol Award and Foreword Magazine's Book of the Year.

She is married to her Prince Charming, a man who thinks she's hilarious—but only when she's not trying to be. Christy is a self-proclaimed klutz, an avid music lover who's known for spontaneously bursting into song, and a road trip aficionado.

When she's not working or spending time with her family, she enjoys singing, playing the guitar, and exploring small, unsuspecting towns where people have no idea how accident-prone she is.

Find Christy online at:
www.christybarritt.com
www.facebook.com/christybarritt
www.twitter.com/cbarritt

Sign up for Christy's newsletter to get information on all of her latest releases here: **www.christybarritt. com/newsletter-sign-up/**